J. Perkins Tracy, Napoleon Sarony

The Blockade Runner

J. Perkins Tracy, Napoleon Sarony

The Blockade Runner

ISBN/EAN: 9783337376598

Printed in Europe, USA, Canada, Australia, Japan

Cover: Foto ©Andreas Hilbeck / pixelio.de

More available books at **www.hansebooks.com**

The Blockade Runner

BY

J. PERKINS TRACY

AUTHOR OF

"The Heart of Virginia," "Won by the Sword," etc.

STREET & SMITH CORPORATION

PUBLISHERS

79-89 Seventh Avenue, New York

THE BLOCKADE RUNNER.

CHAPTER I.

THE BLOCKADE RUNNER.

" WHAT are our chances of getting into Wilmington to-night, cap'n ?"

The speaker, a fine, handsome young fellow of twenty-five, attired in a thick pea-jacket, dark blue trowsers and undress naval cap, had just come on the quarterdeck from the cabin of the steamer Foxhound.

" Good," was Captain Powell's brief reply.

He held his mouth close to the young man's ear so that the word should not be blown back down his throat.

A heavy winter's gale was shrieking through the rigging of the vessel, and the dark sea was running furiously.

She was steaming comparatively slowly, head on to the billows, while Foulweather Tom, the pilot, on whom rested the responsibility of taking her over the bar, was the picture of anxious watchfulness.

The steamer was wrapped in darkness from stem to stern—not the gleam of a lantern visible, and the binacle light was completely shaded.

" It's a snorter—this night is," said the young man presently, turning his back against the wind.

The skipper did not immediately reply, for a terrible gust just then swept the deck, sending a quantity of cold spray into his face, and a chill along his bones.

"It's a regular January blow," he shouted at length, his cheeks puffing out like a pair of bellows.

"Seen any gun boats?"

"Nary one," replied the captain. "They're pretty well scattered to-night, I reckon, and we are not likely to be seen at all, unless we run afoul of one of them ourselves."

He turned red in the face from the exertion of talking.

"Come below, Mr. Bentham. I'm chilled to the bone and must have a bracer. We can't talk here."

The pair at once dived down the companion way.

Captain Powell wiped the tiny icicles from his beard and eyebrows, and the moisture from his mahogany-hued cheeks.

He then mixed two glasses of stiff grog, and pushing one toward his companion, gulped down the contents of the other with evident relish.

"Yes," said the skipper complacently, "we will make port safely this time. It is just the kind of night for it—black as ink and blowing great guns. You feel how the old gal rises to the sea—and she's as dry as a bone. I had her thoroughly overhauled and freshly caulked at Cherbourg, for I knew what I might expect off this coast at this time of the year. Some of those leaky tubs that try to run the blockade would founder in this gale."

"I should say the Foxhound is a stanch craft," replied young Bentham. "I have been impressed with her seagoing qualities since I took passage on board.

She's got such a reputation that I fancy Uncle Sam would be glad to overhaul her."

" You can take your davy to that, Mr. Bentham," said the skipper with a grin, " but he won't have that pleasure this trip, nor for many more trips, if I can help it. Foulweather Tom is the crack pilot in this business, and the Foxhound has a mortgage on his services. What he don't know about the channels and shoals and sand bars off Charleston and Wilmington, as well as the Georgia coast, ain't worth considering. There's two channels into Wilmington, where we're bound—the bar channel and the beach channel—and if you don't keep your weather eye lifting on a night such as this the chances are you run hard and fast on to the middle ground, and with such a sea running you'd go to pieces in no time."

" That would be pleasant certainly."

" I reckon you might say your prayers, if you know any. Have another tot of grog."

" Thanks, not any more," said Bentham.

" You must be aware the Yankee fleet has a big job on its hands when it undertakes to blockade Wilmington," said the bronzed old sea-dog while he mixed himself a second potation. " When the wind blows off the coast, the vessels are forced to sea and scattered ; when it turns and blows landward they are compelled to haul off to escape the awful sea. For six months in the year it is next to impossible for a vessel to lie at anchor safely off the Carolina coast. So you see that everything is in our favor."

" I'm glad to hear it," said the young man.

" This gale is a little worse, if anything, than the one that took us in with our last cargo. Then we were laden with shoes, blankets, caps and blouses for the graycoats; now, our hold is stored with muskets, sabers, percussion caps and such things, besides a quantity of quinine, the most valuable thing of all."

" Worth about——"

" The whole cargo ?"

" Yes."

" Say about three millions."

The passenger started, and seemed to meditate for a moment.

" Oh, we carry richer cargoes than this sometimes," continued the captain, mistaking meditation for amazement. " And the beauty of it all is that we've never lost one."

" The pitcher which goes often to the well gets broken at last, you know," said Bentham, smiling.

" There are exceptions to every rule," said Captain Powell, " and the Foxhound is fast proving that adage a downright humbug. Do you know, sir, that this is my eighth successful run ?"

" You astonish me."

" Fact, sir. This steamer has paid for herself several times over, for the profits are enormous."

" So I have heard."

" I shall fill up to the hatches with cotton, which stands us in about eight cents a pound. How much do you think it will fetch at Liverpool ?"

" I haven't the slightest idea," said Bentham, though he knew very well that the price of that material in Europe was extremely high.

" About four shilllings a pound," replied the skipper, smacking his lips with great gusto, as though the mere mention of that figure was like an agreeable morsel on the tongue.

" I don't wonder this war enriches some people very fast," said the young man thoughtfully.

" I should say it does. Why, sir, there are people, to my knowledge, who are now riding about in their carriages, that a year—ay, six months ago—were comparatively paupers. What was Nassau before the war? The inhabitants were chiefly wreckers and fishermen, and but few vessels lay along the wharves or rode in the offing. Look at the place to-day! The harbor is alive with shipping, and its wharves are crowded with cotton bales awaiting transportation to Europe, as well as merchandise, contraband of war, ready to be shipped for the blockaded Southern ports. It is the chief depot for the traffic. Confederate agents are established there, and the town has expanded into a port of immense importance."

Captain Powell's passenger listened but said nothing.

" You understand that the Bahamas, being a British possession, the Yankee cruisers cannot effect a legal capture within the three-mile limit, so they are forced to take their station off Abaco Light, and run their chance. The blockade runners generally await a dark and foggy night for getting away, and as we are careful to show no lights, you may easily judge that the cruisers have no sinecure trying to catch us."

" It is unusual for a blockade runner to go direct to Europe and then return with a contraband cargo, as you have lately done, isn't it, cap'n ?" said Bentham.

" Yes. Most of these vessels are light-draught steamers built expressly for the trade, and intended only to make the trip, either from Bermuda, Nassau or Cuba. The Foxhound is a superior vessel, and the owners, of which I am one, had reasons for assuming an unusually hazardous risk. I shall not repeat the venture, at least not very soon. Had you not run foul of me at Cherbourg, Mr. Bentham, you would not likely have made this voyage direct. You would have been obliged to take passage for one of the places I have just named and there transhipped."

"I consider myself fortunate in having secured passage in the Foxhound, the more especially as she is a lucky vessel."

"Ay, ay; but you'll have to excuse me now, as I judge we are approaching dangerous ground. If I were you, sir, I'd remain below. It's a deal sight cosier than on deck such a night as this."

"Thank you; but I don't mind the storm a bit. You know I got my sea legs on long ago."

"Well, please yourself."

Captain Powell stalked up the brass-bound staircase facing the wheel, his passenger close at his heels.

As they emerged from their shelter the wind almost took them off their feet, and the icy spray blown aft, as it continually came over the bows of the steamer, struck their faces like cold kisses from the depths of the sea.

It was the night of —th of January, 1862, and one of the wildest storms that swept the North Carolina coast during war times was then at its height.

The Foxhound was not the only vessel abroad in the gale.

Toward sundown a strong easterly wind had met the ebb-tide, and the whole coast presented a terrible appearance.

The fleet of Federal blockaders, which for months

had confronted Wilmington with their grim guns, was compelled to seek safety in the offing, for to remain near the coast would prove certain destruction.

Added to the wind, that blew with tremendous force, was a perfect hailstorm of sleet, that cut the darkness like Scythian arrows.

Besides, the cold was enough to freeze any one at the helm.

The Foxhound steadily pursued her way.

Time and again she had successfully run the blockade, and Captain Powell did not believe that there could be a break in his former good luck.

She was an English-built craft, a remarkably swift one, and so arranged that she could navigate the seas with or without steam.

She carried no armament aside from her officers' private weapons.

Her *forte* was flight, not resistance, and there was not in the Federal service at that time a vessel swift enough to overhaul her.

Time and again she had been chased on the high seas, but always outwitted her hunters.

She was well known to the Union fleet, by which she was constantly watched.

Her cargoes were always sure to be of great value to the Confederacy; and on the night mentioned above she carried one worth, as her captain has said, three million dollars.

Not three millions in Confederate bills, but in hard, glittering gold.

The passenger resolutely facing the wintry gale on the wet decks of the trim blockade runner was a man who had boarded her at Cherbourg, from whence she had sailed bound for Wilmington.

He was a young man named Robert Bentham, an American by birth, and a person who seemed to know a good deal about ship gunnery.

Indeed, he had been educated at one of the best naval schools in France, and was on his way to take part in the terrible conflict raging between the two sections of the Union.

On which side?

Why ask the question, when we find him a passenger on board a Confederate blockade runner, and almost in port?

If his sympathies were with the Union, why did he not take passage in a vessel bound for New York?

Let the future pages of our romance solve these questions.

For some time the Foxhound kept steadily on her course, breasting the terrible waves with her cutting prow, and guided all the time by the sailor at the wheel.

Captain Powell knew that the storm had beaten the Federal blockaders off the coast.

But his experience also taught him that the gunboats kept a particularly argus-eyed watch on such nights as this, as it offered a favorable chance for the low-lying lead-painted blockade runners to elude the squadron.

In spite of the assertion he had made to his passenger of a safe and speedy run, he was fully alive to the dangers that beset him as he drew in near the shore.

He could not tell what moment he might run foul of a gunboat.

He knew the crews were kept ready at their stations

for every emergency, and that a sudden and well-directed broadside would cripple if not sink the Fox-hound at a most unexpected juncture.

The squadron steamed about as close in shore as they dared, and now every instant was fraught with the greatest peril.

With an anxious face, and eyes trying to pierce the night, he stood on deck watching the course of his gallant ship, as she pressed on through the awful seas that seemed always to ingulf her.

His beard was a mass of ice, but he did not mind the cold and the storm.

All at once there rose between him and the swelling sea a huge object, darker than the night itself.

Captain Powell sprang toward the wheel, with an exclamation struggling to his lips.

"I see it, sir," said Foulweather Tom, before the captain could speak. "It is a Yankee blockader. Hard a-port!" he said softly to the helmsman.

The wheel spun around and the Foxhound sheered off within a biscuit-toss of the dangerous object.

It was a moment of intense anxiety to all on deck.

CHAPTER II.

AN AWFUL PROJECT.

BRAVE as he was, Captain Ralph Powell held his breath from fear.

Every second he expected to see her ports fly open, and her guns open fire ; and his strained imagination pictured the ripping and tearing sound of the wooden hull of his steamer under the hail of iron missiles.

The terrible suspense really only lasted for a brief interval, and then the Foxhound was running under the blockader's bows like a phantom.

She soon left the gunboat in her wake, a blot on the water, from which it vanished as the distance between the two vessels increased.

" A narrow shave, by George !" exclaimed the skipper softly, drawing a long breath.

" Ay, ay, sir," responded the pilot, calmly resuming his position by the weather rail.

With the salty sleet blowing like hailstones in his eyes, and flogging his weather-beaten cheeks, Foulweather Tom clung to his post and peered into the blackness ahead, fully conscious that he was doing his duty.

It was now about two bells, or one o'clock in the morning, though of course the bells were not struck.

The captain went on the bridge, followed by his

passenger, and Foulweather Tom followed after a time.

"What's that just for'ard of the port beam, cap'n?" said Bentham suddenly, pointing to a spot a little darker, if that were possible, than the surrounding water.

"By gum! A gunboat!"

Powell's eyes seemed about to leap from their sockets.

"And yonder," ejaculated Bentham excitedly, "is a second one."

"We are running into the midst of the Yankee squadron," exclaimed the skipper, jumping toward the pilot.

"Vessels straight ahead and off our bows, Tom," he said.

"I know it, captain."

"We are in a dangerous place."

"That's so, sir."

The coolness of the pilot argued well for the success of the expedition.

For a few moments longer the Foxhound kept portward, when all at once a rocket shot upward, apparently from the very depths of the sea, and exploded above the masts of the largest vessel.

An oath fell from Powell's lips as the rocket burst.

"Discovered! Now we're in for it!" he said with compressed lips.

The Federal signal told him that they had, indeed, reached the most dangerous part of the voyage.

A minute later several responsive rockets soared heavenward, revealing the position of as many Union blockaders to the captain.

"Go ahead full speed, cap'n," said Foulweather Tom.

Powell returned to the center of the bridge and signalled the engineer.

The Foxhound, which for some time had been running at half-speed, now bounded forward, like her namesake, after a quarry.

"Steady a-starboard!" whispered the pilot, and the word was instantly passed to the man at the wheel.

The words had scarcely left his mouth ere the flash of a cannon lit up a part of the sea for a moment, and a shot tore across the Foxhound's deck, carrying a piece of the taffrail into the sea.

"That Yankee gunner must have the eyes of an owl!" said Powell, amazed at the shot. "The next one will pierce our counter, and the next tear through our boiler-room."

Lights seemed to be flashing on every side, but darkness still enveloped the blockade runner.

Her crew knew the danger and swarmed her deck, but not a loud word was spoken.

Hard upon the first shot from the Union fleet came another and another, only one of which took effect, with a crash of splintering wood, in the hull of the steamer.

"Hard a-starboard!" said Foulweather Tom.

"Hard down she is," came back the word.

Another bright flash and another shot tore a jagged piece out of the mizzen-mast.

Evidently the Union gunners, in spite of the rough sea, which rendered an accurate aim almost impossible, were well up in their line of work.

Things were getting decidedly **warm, but the**

steamer was drawing inside the line of blockaders fast; but she was liable to be disabled before she succeeded in getting out of range.

Captain Powell stood with hands clinched and a face reddened by madness.

Presently a broadside was fired from a point where no vessel had yet been seen, and the iron balls tore like hail across the Foxhound's deck, killing two sailors and knocking the smokestack away.

Gun after gun now opened on the devoted little blockade runner; but the man at the helm did his duty, and the ship kept on regardless of the iron shower.

It was now a race for life, and every minute was that much precious time.

Bentham, the young passenger, had not left his post for a moment.

He stood erect like a person without fear, watching the flash of the Federal guns with the utmost nonchalance imaginable.

Foulweather Tom had reached a pathway leading straight to port; but the Union fleet seemed determined to sink him outside the bar.

"Look yonder," exclaimed Powell. "Do you see that gunboat? They are going to get between us and the shoals. There! there is a mountain of iron straight ahead! I guess the days of the Foxhound are numbered. Well, if it comes to the worst, I know what to do. If I cannot escape I will keep my oath. I will reach port or perish!"

Powell had scarcely finished ere the flash of a heavy gun illuminated a point dead ahead, and a shot hummed across the deck fore-and-aft, so near the skipper's head that he fairly staggered, and grasped the rail of the bridge to save himself.

"We're done for!" he exclaimed wildly. "But they shan't take me. I'll go to the bottom first!"

With a bound Powell sprang to the deck and rushed below.

"Hard a-port!" screamed the pilot.

"What does the cap'n mean?" Bentham said to the pilot.

"Dunno," replied Foulweather Tom. "What did he say?"

"Swore all was up, and that he'd send the Fox-hound to the bottom before he'd be taken."

"Then for God's sake follow and stop him!" exclaimed the man. "We carry a torpedo in the hold, and a fuse runs to the cap'n's stateroom. The skipper is stark, staring mad! All's not lost yet. Stop him quick, or we shall all be sent to Davy Jones in a flash."

"Great heavens!" exclaimed Bentham, his cheek paling at the awful possibility. "He is mad, surely. He must not be permitted to carry out his fearful purpose."

The next minute he was descending the companion-way after the reckless captain.

It was a moment big with the fate of the noble vessel and fifty valuable lives.

The swing of the vessel as she rolled to the boiling seas threw Bentham forward on his hands and knees upon the cabin floor.

He sprang to his feet and looked about.

There was no sign of Captain Powell.

His stateroom door was ajar, however, and the pas-senger ran to it and pushed it open.

The sight he saw he felt he never would forget.

The skipper crouched on the deck with a lighted lantern in front of him, the slide open.

In his hand he held one end of a dark-looking snake-like rope, which issued from beneath his berth.

He was unraveling a bit of yarn which protected the end of the fuse, preparatory to applying the candle-light.

Crash !

A round shot came tearing through the vessel's side, dashing the lantern into a hundred fractures, and ripping a great hole in the woodwork in its course athwart the deck, smashing things generally in the cabin beyond, and shattering an exit to the sea.

Powell, wrapped in sudden darkness, uttered a fearful oath.

Bentham stood back aghast.

He could feel the tremble of the deck from the rapid throb of the engines, for the Foxhound was driving ahead at her utmost speed, the firemen below piling on tar and rosin, until the pitching and rolling fabric shook as with the ague.

It was an awful moment.

The huge waves thundered against the steamer's sides as if determined to hinder her escape from the lawful guardians of the port.

The wind whistled down the cabin stairs, and a hundred odd noises added to the tumult of the hour.

Bentham saw the flash of a match in the darkness, and the captain's face, looking fairly demoniacal, was lit up by the illumination.

Only for a moment, then a draught of cold air through the shot-hole extinguished the flame.

Another curse from the skipper, followed almost immediately by a fearful crash on deck.

Another solid shot had taken effect, but the vessel's speed was unchecked.

The frenzied captain struck another match, but like the first it puffed out.

As he struck the third, Bentham stepped forward and took him by the shoulder.

The match fell and was extinguished, while Powell sprang to his feet.

The two men faced each other in utter gloom.

" Who are you ?" demanded the skipper with an imprecation.

" Bentham."

" What are you doing here ?"

" To save you from a crime."

" Curse you, what do you mean ?"

" I mean that I have just learned of the existence of a torpedo in the hold of this steamer, and of your purpose to fire it sooner than surrender to the cruisers. You are mad, cap'n !"

" How dare you dictate to me !"

" You must not destroy this vessel."

" *Must* not ?" hissed Powell.

" Must not !" said Bentham calmly. " We are not yet stopped. Escape is still possible. We are almost over the bar. Your pilot will take her in, if there be the ghost of a chance."

" We are doomed," yelled the skipper, " and I'm going to rob the Yankees of their prey. Their flag shall never float over the Foxhound. I have sworn it, and mean to keep my oath !"

" You are beside yourself, man," said Bentham. " We are not yet disabled."

"Hark! Do you hear that?" cried Powell, as another shot smashed the cabin bulkhead.

"Well," said his passenger coolly, "let them sink us if they can. We shall then go to the bottom without the aid of your infernal machine. If you were calmer you'd know they can never board us in this sea. If the machinery is hit, we shall drift ashore and go to pieces. In no case will the gunboats take possession."

The passenger's logic was undeniable, but Powell had only one idea in his brain, and was deaf to reason or entreaty.

He had sworn to blow the Foxhound to atoms some day, and the mania was in complete control of his senses.

"You are insane, cap'n, and I will not permit you to execute your project."

With an oath Powell sprang upon his passenger, and an awful struggle in the dark ensued.

CHAPTER III.

THE FOXHOUND ARRIVES IN PORT.

BENTHAM was a wiry, athletic young fellow, but Powell was a man of powerful physique, and was moreover actuated by a desperate resolve.

The passenger went down under the fierce assault, and he felt the skipper grappling for his throat.

The young fellow exerted all his strength, and by a quick movement rolled the captain over and straddled him.

Then he had his hands full trying to keep his assailant under.

The struggle continued several moments, with a fearful exertion of muscle and determination on the part of each, but Bentham succeeded in maintaining his advantage.

At last the captain desisted and remained passive.

Evidently he was gathering his breath and energies for a fresh attempt to displace his adversary.

"Why can't you be sensible, Powell?" said Bentham, puffing out the words. "Don't you see we're still under way. Not a shot has struck us in the last five minutes. If you go on deck I'll bet you'll find us in the beach channel, running up under the guns of Fort Caswell."

Powell made no reply.

"Look here. I've a revolver in my hand now. If

you don't give up this insane freak of yours there'll be blood shed."

At that instant a sailor flashed a lantern into the stateroom, and Captain Powell saw the gleam of a pistol barrel, and the stern realization seemed to bring him to his senses.

"Let me up!" he growled.

"Will you go on deck if I do?"

"Yes—darn you; since you've got the drop on me. I can't help myself."

Bentham released the prostrate skipper.

"Give me that lantern," said the young man to the sailor. "How are things on deck?"

"We're in the channel, sir."

"And the gunboats?"

"Astern and out of range, sir."

"Then we're safe?"

"Ay, ay; so the pilot says."

"What have you got to say, Captain Powell?" said Bentham.

"What!" exclaimed the skipper, who had regained his mental equilibrium; "why, that you've saved the steamer, my boy, and there's my hand on it."

They clasped hands heartily.

"The pilot sent me below to find you, sir," said the seaman to his superior.

"All right, Ducks, tell him I'll be up in a jiffy."

The sailor hurried away.

"Allow me to say, Bentham, that you're a brick. Your intrepidity has saved vessel, crew and cargo from certain destruction. I hope you will accept my apology for my rough treatment. I was not really conscious of anything but the one determination to blow this craft to the four winds of heaven. I've had it so long on my mind, and the wind of that cannon-ball turned my head, so that I could think only that the time had arrived for putting my last resource into execution."

"Say no more, Captain Powell."

"But I assure you I'm heartily ashamed of myself. How came you to.learn about the torpedo? I never told you."

"The pilot——"

"Ay, ay; Foulweather Tom knows all about it. Some day, however, I'll be obliged to carry it into effect. You've seen the legend painted over the cabin door: 'This steamer will never be taken by the enemy.' That's my motto, and I mean to stick by it. Wouldn't the Yankees chaff me if they could run their flag up to the mizzen-peak? Do you think I could stand that? Never!"

"Well, sir, you're captain and part owner of this craft, and are in a position to do as it pleases you.; but let me tell you that such a project as you have in view is, in my opinion, a crime of the first magnitude. Every man who ships aboard the Foxhound has the sword of Damocles suspended above his head with a very slender thread. It is simply a foolhardy trick to destroy vessel and crew, and yourself, too, for that matter, in order to carry out a vainglorious threat. You'll excuse me, Captain Powell, but I can't help telling you what I think of your method."

"I shall not quarrel with your opinion, Bentham. You've a perfect right to it. The people of Wilmington, however, shall know that you've saved three million dollars' worth of war material to the Confederacy."

" I beg you will not mention it, sir."

" What!" exclaimed Powell, incredulously " Not mention it? Why, man, they'll give you a public ovation!"

" I prefer not to have the notoriety."

" Do you really mean that?"

" I do; and I request as a favor that you will say nothing about my agency in this affair. Remember, it would only reflect on yourself."

" That's so," admitted Powell; "I didn't think of that. I won't say a word, then. Hold the light till I put the fuse away. There now, we'll go on deck."

They passed from the stateroom and ascended the stairs

The Foxhound was running in by the beach channel, and the frowning battlements of Fort Caswell could be just distinguished off the starboard bow in the gloom.

Foulweather Tom was on the bridge and had just signalled to the engine-room to reduce speed, for the blockade runner was out of danger from the gunboats.

They had ceased firing and were steaming off shore, though their iron hulls were no longer visible to the Foxhound's people.

" Safe at last, eh, Tom?" exclaimed the skipper, who was now in an exhilarating mood.

" I see you thought better of blowing us all to kingdom come," replied the pilot.

" If I failed it is because of the interference of our passenger. He is a gallant fellow, and deserves the thanks of all on board," said Powell, in a low voice.

" Ay, ay; I believe you, sir," answered Foulweather Tom.

All at once there was a concussion, followed by a shiver through the steamer that jarred every one on board.

"We're aground!" cried Captain Powell. "You've run too close to the Middle Ground, Tom."

The pilot, without a word, sprang to the center of the bridge and signalled the engineer to go ahead at full speed; at the same moment a great wave lifted the Foxhound, and she slid forward over the obstruction into deep water again.

"The sand has shifted at that point," said Foulweather Tom, as he again signalled to slow down.

Fifteen minutes more and the distant lights of Wilmington hove into view.

"Ha!" exclaimed Powell exultantly, "yonder's the city. Bentham, the Confederacy owes you a debt of gratitude. If you had not shipped with us, by thunder, we would all have been food for the fishes at this moment, and a cargo of inestimable value would be lying at the bottom of the sea. What an infernal idiot I was! Five minutes more and you would have been too late. Next time I'll look before I leap."

The young man looked very thoughtful.

Just then four bells were struck forward.

Two o'clock in the morning.

The tempest was still having things pretty much its own way, and the standing rigging of the vessel was incrusted with icicles.

The mizzen-mast had been shot away, leaving only a jagged stump.

The taffrail was demolished in several places along the quarter-deck.

Half of the smokestack was gone and the balance

above deck in ruins, so that the black smoke blew shoreward on a level with the shattered bulwarks.

The boats at the davits were perfect wrecks.

Indeed, the Foxhound had been terribly cut up, and had many nasty-looking shot-holes in her hull.

But her machinery had escaped injury; one shot in the engine-room would most likely have settled her fate for good and all.

Near on to six bells the blockade runner had come to anchor close in shore, ready to steam up to her dock after sunrise.

The good people of Wilmington slept in ignorance of the arrival of a cargo of precious freight, but the newspapers were already preparing accounts under flaring headlines of her wonderful escape, for the news had been long since telegraphed from Fort Caswell, and reporters had flocked down the bay and boarded her almost as soon as the night lights of the city sprang into view.

By eight o'clock in the morning the Foxhound was moored to her dock, and a large crowd was already gathered to survey the ruin wrought by the Yankee gunners.

By this time the news of her arrival and thrilling experience was all over the city, and a stream of curiosity seekers and patriotic idlers were *en route* for the dock.

The scene on the wharf beggared description.

Men shouted and danced for very joy, and women waved their handkerchiefs and joined their voices to the loud cheers that soared skyward.

The city bells were set a-ringing, and whistles were tooted, until there was not a soul, young or old, in the city but knew that the famous Foxhound, with her equally famous skipper, Powell, had arrived all the way from Cherbourg, France, with a valuable cargo.

Extras sold like wildfire, and everybody was talking to somebody else on the streets, whether he had ever met the individual before or not.

Conventionalities were for the time done away with, and people could hardly contain themselves.

After breakfast, Bentham left the Foxhound and elbowed his way through the crowd, an object of envy to the men and admiration to the women—for every man who had come in on the blockade runner was a hero in the eyes of the enthusiastic multitude.

"May I never have to deal with another madman like Captain Powell," he said to himself. "One of these days he'll blow his vessel to the winds. Well, I know one man who won't shed tears if he does," and the young stranger smiled to himself. "I didn't do the Union a service when I saved the Foxhound's cargo. I was looking to Bob Bentham's interest just then. I didn't relish the idea of going starward on a piece of a torpedo. Yet I may make such an uncomfortable trip one of these days, if I take a hand in this war, as I propose doing. The city *does* look a bit changed during my three years' absence. However, that doesn't matter, I can find my way to Uncle Gordon Mowbray's without any difficulty; and if my plans don't miscarry I shall soon shake the Wilmington dust from my shoes, and in a way I am afraid won't please my respected relative."

Just then he was approached by a handsome elderly gentleman, in faultless attire, and with iron gray whiskers—a person whose appearance would have at once established his position in life as one of wealth and importance.

"Welcome, my dear boy!" he exclaimed, grasping Bentham's hand with great cordiality. "I assure you I'm delighted to see you once more in Wilmington. You've come with great *éclat.* Your name is in the papers as a distinguished passenger on the lucky Fox-hound. Do you know, Robert, I'm quite proud of you, and so is Norah."

"Thank you, uncle; you've not changed a bit unless it is for the better," said the young man.

"You had a tight squeeze it seems getting through the Yankee fleet, this morning. Thank fortune that the Foxhound's star is still in the ascendant. She's had so many escapes since she started into the trade that I verily believe old Powell has the devil's own luck. A cargo worth three millions, and direct from Europe, too; well, well, it's certainly a wonderful record even for the Foxhound."

"Yes, uncle, we had a hard run for it—and at one time were in greater peril than you could imagine."

"I don't doubt it, my dear boy. We've been look-ing for you these two weeks. Norah got your letter, saying that you would sail in the Foxhound; but we were getting nervous lest you had been gobbled up by a Yankee cruiser. By Jove, my dear boy, you're look-ing well, and you've come back in the nick of time. The South needs such men as you are just now."

Bentham's brow darkened at the last sentence, and he avoided the speaker's gaze.

"Here's the carriage. I'll send the man back for your trunk. Jump in."

Uncle and nephew entered the family vehicle and drove off toward the fashionable quarter of the town.

CHAPTER IV.

SHORT BUT SIGNIFICANT.

ONLY two persons of all the crowd on the wharf followed the movements of Mr. Mowbray and Robert Bentham.

One was a dapper-looking young man of thirty, with piercing dark eyes, regular features that might be considered handsome, but which gave some evidence of fashionable dissipation.

A physiognomist would rather have distrusted his face, discerning craft and dissimulation in every line.

His chin and mouth showed dogged resolution and stubbornness.

Altogether it could not be termed a pleasing countenance, though there was no doubt of the indications of latent energy that characterizes a successful business man.

He was known to his intimates as Flash Gilmor.

His companion was younger, much handsomer, but weak and listless, as though he took the world easy, and possessed no other care than the negative exertion necessary to amuse the passing moment.

"You saw those two men who just drove off, Jessup?" said Gilmor.

"Yes, I saw them," was the reply. "I recognized Mowbray, of course. Everybody knows that old Crœsus."

" The other is that young nephew of his, Bob Bentham."

" You don't say. I've heard of him. Mowbray sent him to France to complete his education. That was before the war. His father, I think, left him quite a tot, and old Crœsus is his guardian."

" Yes. I thought he'd turn up in Wilmington just when I wanted him a thousand miles away. I wish the Yankee fleet had sent him to the bottom of the sea."

" I guess you must hate the fellow pretty heartily to wish him such luck. What has he ever done to you?"

Flash Gilmor glared a moment after the carriage.

" His presence here is a menace to my happiness."

" In what respect, my dear fellow ?" said Jessup.

" Well, it's no great secret that I'm infatuated with Miss Mowbray, the old gentleman's ward. She'll be a great heiress in time, and besides is a deuced pretty girl. She's got a pair of eyes that would turn any fellow's heart, and the figure of a Venus. But her chief recommendation is her expectations. Old Mowbray is well fixed, and I know she'll come in for the bulk of his estate one of these days. Moneys talks every time—especially these times when gold is getting so devilish scarce that a fellow is in danger of forgetting what a double-eagle looks like."

" Ah, very true; these Confederate shinplasters have a fluctuating and uncertain value, I observe, and a man handles them quite gingerly," remarked Jessup with a lazy drawl, as though the financial outlook was rather a bore to him.

" Well, to cut this subject short, Bob Bentham has an eye in the same quarter himself. She was sixteen when he went away to Europe, and as his position as a member of the family brought him continually into her society, I am certain he was impressed, as any young man would be under the circumstances. If that were the case three years ago, just fancy the effect on this young absentee of the full developed charms of one of the most charming women in the world. Why, man alive, it will be a clear case of love at first sight. As he is certain to be backed up by her father, who thinks there is no one like his nephew Bob, where in old Nick do I come in?"

This was too much of a poser for the fallow brain of the easy-going Mr. Jessup to tackle, so he said nothing but sucked the end of his gold-mounted cane assiduously, possibly hoping to find an inspiration by that recreation.

"You perceive how much of a drawback to me is this young fellow's advent in Wilmington just at the important time when I had begun to flatter myself that I was making some progress with Miss Mowbray."

Mr. Jessup nodded wisely, still fondling his cane with his lips.

"I've not the least doubt Bentham will offer his services to the Confederacy, and Mowbray has sufficient influence to obtain for him an important commission. I am not sure but he may go to sea in the privateer Swiftwing."

"The vessel to which you hold the appointment as second officer, eh?" said Mr. Jessup, removing his cane for a moment.

"The same; though between you and I, Jessup, and mind you keep mum about it, I fancy Flash Gilmor will be conspicuous by his absence."

"You don't say?" exclaimed Mr. Jessup, with a sort of mild surprise.

"I only hope the fellow does go to sea in the Swift-wing."

"Pray why? To be shot or taken by the un-gentlemanly Yankees, I suppose."

"Yes, of course ; and for another reàson also," said Gilmor mysteriously. .

"Indeed! What is the other reason?"

"That's a secret at present. I can only hint to you that he's not very likely to come back to trouble one if he *does* go in that vessel."

"Oh!" said Mr. Jessup, opening his eyes, and then returning the knob of the cane to his lips.

"We'll drop the subject, if you please, now. I'm going up to Bardolph Bros. You can go as far as the counting-room door, as it's not out of your way."

"Who are Bardolph Bros., Flash?" said Mr. Jessup, as the pair left the wharf.

"They are the owners of the **steamer Swiftwing.**"

CHAPTER V.

UNCLE AND NEPHEW.

"HERE is the old house, Robert," said Mr. Mowbray to his nephew as the carriage turned into an elegant drive leading up to a fine residence, fronted by grand trees, which through the day threw around a pleasing shade. "I need not announce your arrival to Norah," he continued, "for the papers have told her of the Foxhound's return, and she has expected you on that steamer."

Mowbray had hardly finished when the front door of the mansion opened, and the graceful figure of a young woman appeared on the threshold.

"It is Norah!" whispered Mowbray. "See if she will recognize you."

The next moment the person in the doorway sprung airily toward the two men.

"The Foxhound brought him, I see," she said, glancing at Mowbray as she held out her hands to the young man. "Welcome—welcome to the old home, Robert. The three years have been three ages; but the last one has ended at last."

The lighting up of Bentham's eyes told how this reception pleased him, and a thrill of delight shot through his heart while he held the girl's hands in his, and gazed into her deep, honest eyes.

Still holding one of her hands, he passed into the

house whose threshold he had not crossed for three years.

Gordon Mowbray was a widower. His wife left him childless when she died, but the girl, Norah, whom he had adopted, was the light of his elegant home. He loved her with the affection of a father, and we need not say that his love was returned.

Everybody knew that Norah was not his child, but few knew that her true name was Norah Narcross, for she was everywhere known as Norah Mowbray, a name which had been given her by common consent.

When Robert Bentham went to the continent for the purpose of completing his education, he left Norah a beautiful girl of sixteen, one of the belles of Wilmington, and a lass with the purest of hearts.

His home-coming, for Gordon Mowbray's house was really his home, his parents being dead, found her a woman of nineteen arrayed in the garments of a riper beauty, with a deeper, softer blue in her eyes and the carriage of a queen.

He stood in the presence of a woman fairer than any he had seen in France.

"You must have had an exciting time coming in," said Norah, when young Bentham had taken a seat at her side in the parlor.

"No doubt of that," answered Bentham. "We were hotly chased and badly cut up by cannon-shot, but fortunately we possessed the best of pilots, and I am here, and not at the bottom of the sea."

"For which we are truly thankful, my boy," said Mowbray himself at this juncture. "The Foxhound's cargo is one sorely needed at this time by the South. Several regiments are awaiting arms, and we can now send them to the field. Of course you have képt track of the war?"

"As well as I could," answered Bentham. "I learned a good deal from Captain Powell during the voyage over."

"How do they regard our cause in France?" inquired Mr. Mowbray.

"I heard the war frequently discussed," was the young man's evasive answer.

"What do they say over there about recognition?" asked Mowbray pointedly.

"One party in France favors it——"

"The party nearest the throne?"

"Yes."

"Then it will come. Louis Napoleon wants a foothold in Mexico; we all know that, and he knows on which side his bread's buttered. He will take the initiative step, then England will come handsomely to our rescue, and the war will speedily close."

"Are these not air-castles, uncle?" asked Bentham seriously, and in a tone that riveted the gaze of his two auditors upon him.

"How so, sir?"

"Do you not underrate the resources—the courage of the North?"

"I think not," was the quick and haughty reply. "We know what the Yankee soldiers are. They have been tried. You have read of the rout at Bull Run?"

"I have," said Bentham, coloring slightly; "and I know that the defeat of their army there is a blow which the Federals cannot conceal. But do we not judge them hastily? We have just finished the first year of the war."

It was evident that Bentham looked for Mowbray to continue the argument; but, instead of doing so, he threw a secret glance at Norah which sent her from the room.

"Robert, what means your defense of the North?" he asked, moving his chair nearer to his nephew, whom he looked squarely in the face. "I am shocked to hear such words from you. Why, sir, I have obtained for you the second command on board the new privateer Swiftwing, which is almost ready to sail from Wilmington on her mission of destruction. Explain yourself. Have you come back tainted with Yankee sentiments?"

"I will be frank with you, uncle," said Bentham calmly. "I came to Wilmington to see you and Norah, not to serve the Confederacy, for my heart is not with it. You seem to forget that my father was in the employ of the government at the time of his death. If he had lived, he would have taken his stand for the Union. His son must not turn from the principles he espoused, nor from the flag he carried at his masthead. The Confederacy, if it succeeds, must do so without me. I shall leave Wilmington soon for the North."

"Where you will offer your services to the Federal government?"

Mowbray's words was a menace.

"Perhaps," was the answer. "I shall follow my own inclination."

A cloud of anger darkened the Southerner's face.

"After all I have done for you since your father's death!" he exclaimed, springing up in a spasm of rage, while his eyes flashed fire at the strangely calm young man. " Yes, after all I have paid for your schooling, you turn and sting the bosom that warmed you! Ungrateful boy! Did I send you to the continent to be thoroughly educated in gunnery in order that you might train cannon against the South some day? No! a thousand times no!"

" I am sorry, uncle, that we disagree on so vital a subject. I do not wish to antagonize you, and that, too, on the very day of my arrival; but it is impossible for me to render any service to the Southern Confederacy as my feelings now stand."

" May I ask, sir, who has contaminated those principles on which I have relied? Were you not born in Wilmington? Are you not a true Southerner, body and soul, sir? What is the meaning of this change? Am I to see my own brother's child—my own flesh and blood—turn traitor to the cause which should be nearest his heart?"

" No one has influenced my decision, sir. The principles I avow to you originated solely with myself. I do not agree with the stand taken by the South. I think the issues involved should have been settled by arbitration and not by a recourse to arms. I do not wish you to infer that I think our people are wholly wrong, or that the national government is entirely right. That were too complex a subject for you and I, uncle, to argue upon just now. We had better drop the matter here, lest it lead to a quarrel, which I certainly do not desire."

" Why con——"

" Pray restrain yourself, uncle. Remember, you are my guardian and my father's brother. My love and respect are yours, and ever will be; but do not ask me to act contrary to my inclination. I could not do that even to please you."

"You are an ungrateful cub, sir!" exclaimed the irate Southerner.

"I suppose I am anything you are pleased to call me. But one moment just here," said the young fellow seriously. "You have mentioned the expense connected with my foreign schooling. I am ready to return them with interest. During my sojourn on the continent I have not been idle. I have translated several French naval books into English, and my American publishers have allowed me enough for my trouble to cancel all my obligations to you. You know that my schooling in this country came out of my father's estate."

Mowbray was dumfounded.

His look became a stare; he seemed to recoil from his nephew.

"I presume I am to understand that you refuse the commission I have secured for you as chief officer on the privateer Swiftwing?"

"Yes, sir."

"And you dare insult me by offering to reimburse me for money I have willingly spent on your behalf— money, I regret to say, that has been turned against myself and the cause I uphold?"

"I should prefer not to be under any obligation to you, uncle. Pardon me if I say this, but it is the family pride, and therefore a part of my established principles. You yourself, sir, taught me this."

"I did, sir; but that was when I was ignorant that I was warming a viper in my bosom."

"**That is a hard word, uncle.**"

"But not more than your conduct deserves. I will accept nothing at your hands!" exclaimed Mr. Mowbray. "You have blighted my brightest hopes. Everywhere during the last six months I have sounded your praise, and fame has opened her doors to you. All Wilmington has been waiting for you with an eagerness almost equal to my own. The city stands ready to welcome you, for I am honored here, and there are many people who remember you. But all this comes to an end! I must go out with a lie withering on my lips. I must write to the government at Richmond that Robert Bentham, from whom the South was expecting so much, has gone over to the Yankees!"

It was a painful moment.

Mowbray played well the rôle of a proud man crushed, for he was the character itself.

"A man should listen to the calls of duty," grated Mowbray, starting up again. "If she has made a traitor out of you, obey her call. Turn the cold shoulder to those who have trusted you—turn your back on the South, and forget that you ever trod her sacred soil. Forget Norah—for I swear to you, young man, that the girl will forget you! You know what I told you when you went away, and you know what I have been looking forward to with pleasure. You need not think of such an event now. Norah shall look elsewhere for a husband, and I will help her find one in a man who has not deserted the South in the hour of need!"

Mowbray's whole frame trembled with anger as he spoke.

A fearless smile played at the corners of Bentham's mouth.

He was still the man who had followed Captain Powell to the cabin of the Foxhound.

"Threats shall not turn me from my purpose," he said calmly. "I came to Wilmington to see you and Norah. I have completed my mission, though I did intend to remain a few days; but since I am looked upon with suspicion and unfriendliness my presence is needed no longer here."

He strode toward the door with the last word still on his lips.

Mowbray did not seek to stop him.

"Remain in Wilmington as long as you find it safe," he said, addressing Bentham. "The secret of your action shall not escape my lips; but, sir, I would advise you to leave the city as soon as possible. The people would mob you if they knew your sentiments. You can make my house your home during your stay here."

"I do not wish to compromise you in any manner," was the reply, as the young man halted for a moment at the door. "I shall take your advice and leave Wilmington at the first opportunity. Good-by, Uncle Gordon."

"Good-by, sir."

Bentham opened the door, stepped across the threshold, and shut the portal behind him!

Mowbray was alone.

"Great heavens! do I dream?" he exclaimed, staring vacantly at the place lately occupied by the loyal nephew. "Can it be that he has gone to espouse the cause of the North—he, my sister's child? My money has educated him for service against the Confederacy! He will train the best guns in the Union navy on our ships of war! The stars and bars will be riddled by his balls! It is terrible—more than I can stand! He shall be detained, even if I have to break my word. He shall not fight against us. By Jove! I will force him to accept the commission I have procured for him."

Terribly excited, Mowbray seized his hat and was about to rush from the house, when a door opened and Norah glided into the room.

"Why, where is Robert?" she asked, sending a look of surprise from the empty chair to Mowbray. "Supper is ready for him, but——"

"He isn't here to taste my food, thank heaven!" interrupted the Southerner. "He has subsisted too long off my bounty already. He has left us forever. Our flag is not his flag. He has gone to join the Yankee navy!"

The color left the young woman's face while Mowbray talked, jerking out his short sentences madly. When he finished she recoiled from him as pale as death.

"Gone—so soon!" she gasped, looking at her guardian. "You cannot mean that!"

"He came here to cut me to the heart with his infernal loyalty to what he styles 'the government!'" cried Mowbray. "I should have locked the door on him and turned him over to the Confederate authorities. I was a fool to let him leave the house at will. By Jove, I will do so yet!"

"You will not——"

"Listen to me, child. Robert Bentham is a traitor. He is no longer nephew of mine. I command you to forget him!"

" Forget, Robert? Father you do not mean that."

" I *do* mean it. You were to marry him if you both came to the understanding. But that is over. Robert Bentham is no longer anything to me or to *you !*"

With his last word Mr. Mowbray hastily left the room and the house, while Norah, with clasped hands and swimming eyes, sank grief-stricken on a chair.

CHAPTER VI.

A SHADY TRANSACTION.

WHEN Flash Gilmor presented himself at the shipping house of Messrs. Bardolph Bros., and sent in his card, he was immediately ushered into the private office of the firm.

"Ah, Gilmor," said the senior Bardolph, "happy to see you. Take a seat."

Flash acknowledged the salutation, nodded to the junior Mr. Bardolph, and took possession of the third chair in the room.

"I presume," ventured the elder Bardolph, "you have called in relation to your appointment as second officer of the Swiftwing. She is almost ready for sea."

"Well," said Flash cautiously, "not exactly. The fact of the matter is I have decided not to accept the berth.

Both partners looked at Gilmor with some surprise, but neither made any reply to this announcement, presuming that the gentleman would offer his own explanation unasked.

"May I ask," said Gilmor pointedly, "if the Swift-wing is not for sale?"

Messrs. Bardolph exchanged a swift glance, and then the elder gentleman, stroking his smoothly shaven face, said :

"Ahem! I will not deny that we have contemplated disposing of our interest in the privateer, but that will not affect any arrangements that we have entered upon with yourself or others. If we find a purchaser the transfer will only be consummated with that distinct understanding;" and the speaker smiled suavely.

"Mr. Gilmor," said the junior Bardolph, "as we have not generally circulated the statement of our desire to part with the Swiftwing—indeed we have not yet fully decided upon that point—would you object to telling us from what source you obtained your information?"

"It is immaterial, I think," said Flash significantly. "As I am not a man to beat about the bush I will say that I am fully cognizant of your reasons for wishing to get rid of an undesirable bit of property."

"Sir!" exclaimed Mr. Bardolph senior.

"You wish me to be more explicit? Very well. When I accepted your offer of the commission appointing me to the privateer, I felt it to be my duty to make a thorough examination of the craft in which I was to risk my precious self, you understand."

Messrs. Bardolph exchanged looks again.

"In my opinion, and my experience in naval architecture is of some value, the Swiftwing is not the craft I should care to sail in."

"Indeed, sir," exclaimed the elder Bardolph brusquely, "Captain Powers, whom we have selected as commander, and who is a thorough sailor and officer, does not take such a view of the vessel. He told me that he considers the Swiftwing an admirable vessel in every respect for the purpose in view."

"Captain Powers has a perfect right to his own view, as I contend I have to mine. Besides, I do not

believe the gentleman has taken more than a super
ficial look at the steamer."

"Excuse me, Mr. Gilmor. but your remarks, to say
the least, hide an insinuation that reflects upon our
house."

"If they do, it is your own fault, Mr. Bardolph. A
few coats of paint, a new stanchion here and there,
and a profusion of fresh gingerbread work, cover a.
good deal of rottenness sometimes.

The elder Bardolph sprang to his feet with an exclamation of rage.

"Did you come here, sir, to insult us ?"

"By no means," replied Flash Gilmor coolly; "whatever arraignment I make of the delinquencies of the
Swiftwing could not possibly insult you, seeing that
it is the truth and was deliberately carried out by you
for a purpose."

"Purpose, sir!" cried the senior Bardolph, quite
purple in the face.

"I stand to the word," said Flash ; "the purpose is
apparent. You have taken a floating coffin, regilded
it, and propose to get it off your hands at a high figure,
during the present excitement."

The elder Bardolph sank back in his chair, white
and speechless.

His rage and consternation were something to
witness.

The junior member, who had turned several colors
during the latter part of the interview, seemed to have
recovered himself, and now came to the rescue.

"You seem to have made a very complete investiga-
tion of the privateer."

"I have, sir," acknowledged Gilmor.

" You also see fit to charge us with a very serious— crime."

" I maintain my assertion."

" May I inquire if you came here simply for the *sole* purpose of telling us this ?"

" That depends."

" On what ?"

" Whether you admit that the Swiftwing was purchased and put into commission with the avowed understanding of parting with her."

" Suppose we do not admit such a preposterous thing ?"

Gilmor shrugged his shoulders.

" Let us understand one another," said the junior partner, starting on a new line of action ; " I am convinced you came here with an object. Now what is it ?"

" You haven't answered my question. I will modify it, however, as I consider it none of my business to inquire into your reasons. Is the Swiftwing for sale ?"

The junior member hesitated a moment, while he seemed to pierce his questioner through and through.

At length he said :

" She is."

" Thank you. What is your price ?"

The firm again exchanged looks.

" Have you a purchaser ?" inquired young Mr. Bardolph.

" Not exactly ; but if you will make it my interest to find one I fancy I can get you a good one."

The cat was out of the bag at last, and the Bardolph Brothers each gave a sigh of relief, and immediately assumed a friendly footing with their visitor.

" Why couldn't you have said so at first ?" said the elder partner.

" Excuse me ; I had my reasons."

" Which we won't discuss," said the junior member quickly. " If Mr. Gilmor can find us a purchaser for the Swiftwing I am sure we will give him a very handsome commission."

" That is what I am after," said Flash bluntly. " Now make your figure."

The firm consulted in low tones.

" What would you say to one hundred and thirty thousand dollars ?" suggested the junior Mr. Bardolph, with a faint smile.

" I should say it was a pretty figure to place upon a rotten hulk," was the cool rejoinder.

Mr. Bardolph frowned.

" That is your only price ?" continued Flash.

" We won't take a cent less than one hundred thousand dollars," said Mr. Bardolph, " and at that figure could allow no commission. If you will try for one hundred and thirty we will give you, in the event that you succeed in making the sale, the sum of—ahem !—twenty thousand dollars. If you get a lower price your commission will be proportionably decreased."

" Very well," said Flash Gilmor, " I'll get all I can."

" Now, Mr. Gilmor," said Mr. Bardolph junior, " I think I voice my brother's thoughts, as well as my own, when I say that it seems very probable you have a party in view whom you believe will take the privateer at the stiff valuation we have put upon her. Is it not so ?"

" I beg you will excuse me, gentlemen. I have a scheme in my head which I propose to work upon ;

beyond stating that fact, any other avowal would be premature."

"Oh, that is all right. Go about this matter in your own way, of course. We would simply suggest that you keep the transaction as quiet as possible."

"I shall certainly do so."

Mr. Bardolph junior got up and went to a cupboard, from which he produced a decanter of choice wines, glasses, and a plate of biscuits.

"Here's to the success of your undertaking, Mr. Gilmor."

The sentiment was drank with mild enthusiasm.

"Twenty thousand dollars is not to be picked up every day," said the junior partner.

"I believe you," said Flash. "At least not by the second officer of even a smart privateer."

This sally provoked a hearty laugh from the two partners.

"There's more in you than we ever suspected," said the junior Mr. Bardolph.

"You flatter me," grinned Flash. "By the way," he continued, "when this transaction leaks out, as it is bound to do, by and by, how do you propose to justify yourselves before the business community?"

"Leave that to us, Mr. Gilmor," said the younger Bardolph, with a wink.

"With pleasure, since you will pocket the greater profit by the arrangement; but it strikes me there will be explanations in order, especially as the commissions, men, supplies, and armament come from the Confederate government. It will look rather queer, won't it, if the Swiftwing founders in the first gale?"

"She may meet a Yankee cruiser before that contingency happens," said Bardolph junior.

"She may; but this is the stormy season. Now, frankly, how long do you think the Swiftwing will float during an ordinary blow?" said Flash, grinning.

"That, Mr. Gilmor, is a state secret."

A broad smile was exchanged, and the interview ended at that point.

CHAPTER VII.

THE DUEL AND THE ESCAPE.

ROBERT BENTHAM had marked out his course and was determined to follow it.

He did not like to leave his uncle's house without saying good-by to Norah.

He might see the girl before leaving Wilmington if his exit was not hastened by certain events not unlikely to occur, and he was sure that she would not upbraid him for his course of action.

Her letters to him during his sojourn in France had not warmly espoused the cause of the Confederacy, and he had not given her any insight to his private feelings or sympathies.

"It will be a long war, uncle says," she wrote him shortly after the breaking out of hostilities. "They (the Confederates) have torn down the old flag which gladdened our eyes so long, and a new flag, not a whit lovelier, has been hoisted in its place."

Bentham knew that Wilmington would prove too hot a place for him if his true sentiments became known to its citizens, and he resolved to depart without delay.

It was now verging on to midnight, and the storm through which the Foxhound had steamed to safety had abated.

A number of people still remained in the streets discussing the arrival of the blockade runner and kindred topics, but no one seemed to notice Bentham as he passed along.

He was proceeding toward the wharf at a smart pace, when he was touched by a hand before he was aware that any one was near.

There was something that smacked of arrest in that touch, and Bentham's hand moved toward a weapon as he turned.

"De Lord bress you, Massa Bob!" exclaimed a coal-black darky. "You'se not goin' away widout sayin' good-by to old Jupe, is you?"

"Of course not, Jupe," said Bentham, giving the negro his hand; "but who told you I was going away?"

"I couldn't help hearin' yer last words at Massa Mowbray's," was the reply. "I ain't an eavesdroppah, Bob, but I happened to pass de window just den, an' I heard a few words dat set me to tinkin'. Dar war an eavesproppah, dough."

"An eavesdropper?" echoed the young man starting.

"I saw 'im creep away jes' as I came up. Ha—ha! de brack rascal tink I didn't know 'im!"

"Who was it, Jupe?"

"Tom, ob course."

"One of Mowbray's negroes?"

"Dat's jes' who he war. He am de nigger what's goin' to sail in de Swiftwing with de young Cap'n Powers when dey git ready. Dat Cap'n Powers is a mighty cute chicken, Massa Bob. · Him been comin' mighty often to Massa Mowbray's while you'se been away ober de water. He's got a heap ob business wid massa, somehow or other. I tink sometimes dat him got his eye on de young missus; but mebbe you'se got de best claim dar, an' so him got no show—yah! yah!"

Jupe's last sentence set Bentham to thinking.

He knew nothing of this Captain Powers who was to command the new privateer almost ready to sail.

It might be true, as the negro hinted, that he had a rival for Norah's hand; but what kind of a looking man was he, and was he really a rival?

"Look hyer, Massa Bob, I didn't stop you to set you tinkin' dat way," resumed the negro, breaking in upon the young man's meditations. "If you'se goin' to leave Wilmington dar's no time to be lost, fo' dar's no tellin' who dat eavesdroppin' nigger's carried his news to. He tinks de world ob Cap'n Powers, b'lieves jes' what he b'lieves, an' is allus huntin' fo' some way to serve him. I don't trust dat nigger, Massa Bob. I hates de new flag, but Tom him likes it. He tole me so himself."

Bentham heard the darky through.

It might be that he was in danger.

What was to be done?

He was forced to put this appeal to Jupe, whom he knew could be trusted. The answer was not delayed.

"You must git to de Yankee fleet!" said Jupe. "De storm am about ober, an' de ships will soon be comin' back to de ole stations. I'se watched 'em so long dat I know just whar dey will be. What's de use ob stayin' hyer a minute longer dan you can help, Massa Bob? Tom, de mean nigger, knows jes' whar to find Cap'n Powers, an'——"

"We will go," said Bentham, unconsciously speaking his resolves aloud. "I long to train some loyal cannon on the Conferate navy. My mission to Wilmington is completed. Nothing need keep me here."

The twain turned away and proceeded at a rapid gait toward the mouth of Cape Fear River.

Jupe led the way with the air of one who was confident of success, and ere long, just beyond the confines of the city, he drew a strong boat from beneath the water, and looked up into Bentham's face with a grin of satisfaction.

"Ob course dis yere boat wasn't hyer by chance," said the negro. "I knowed jes' whar to find it. Mebbe I war savin' it fo' an' emergency like the present one. Anyhow, it am jis' de help we want."

Bentham looked over his shoulder at the lights of Wilmington, and thought of the people he was leaving behind.

His mind went back to beautiful Norah Narcross, who would question his hasty departure, and perhaps charge it against him. They had never exchanged vows of love, yet there seemed to be a secret understanding that they were destined for one another, but the spell might be broken, and from that hour their lives might drift apart, never to meet again on the ocean of life.

The war would keep them separate ; it might prove death for one, sorrow and bitterness for the other.

" We mus' be off, Massa Bob," said the negro. " Dar's no tellin' what Tom's gone an' done. De ribber am wide hyer, an' we kin git through de picket boats if we watch de corners."

Bentham stepped into the boat, followed by his dusky friend, who took up the oars and prepared to push out into the stream.

The night was dark, unrelieved by a single star, and a strong breeze was blowing from the sea.

No longer roared the mad waves over the shoals, or raced like horses through the rocky channels.

The air was cold, so cold that Bentham drew his cap around his head.

"I am ready, Jupe," he said. "Now for the Union fleet!"

A moment later the boat would have left the shore, if two figures had not rushed to the water's edge, and a voice exclaimed :

"Put off if you dare! I am here to see you, Robert Bentham."

"It am Cap'n Powers, Massa Bob," whispered Jupe, who still clutched the oars, as the flash of a lantern illumined the night. "I can send de ole boat out of his reach in a second."

"No," said Bentham, rising and facing the figures on shore. "I am here, Captain Powers. What is it you want of me?"

He stepped from the boat as the last word dropped from his tongue, and throwing open his coat, he displayed a sword and two pistols.

"Just what I wish!" continued the privateersman. "I am here to check your flight to the Yankee fleet, but you are willing to fight?"

"Yes, I am eager to meet you, from what I have heard to-night," was the reply. "If you want a provocation let this prove sufficient!"

Hastily drawing his sword, Bentham struck Powers across the face with the flat side.

An oath of rage fell from the captain's lips as he staggered from the blow.

"Fo' de land's sake, dat war a tellin' lick!" ejaculated Jupe, his eyes glittering like a pair of diamonds. "It's no mo' dan Cap'n Powers deserves' fo' sneakin' 'round arter de young missus so much."

The man who accompanied Powers was muffled to the throat in a thick overcoat, but Jupe recognized him as Flash Gilmor.

Hard upon the blow with the flattened side of the sword, Powers drew the weapon that hung in its scabbard on his thigh, and handed the lantern to his friend.

"We will fight here—now!" he exclaimed, facing Bentham, who was already on guard. "That black traitor is your second, I suppose. Gilmor, here, is mine. You were to have been my second officer on the decks of the Swiftwing; but the hopes of many are to be dissipated here. We have never met before, I believe. After this duel we will never meet again."

Bentham did not deign to reply to the boast contained in the last sentence.

His look told that he was eager for the fight.

Gilmor gave the signal, and the next instant fire flashed along the crossed blades.

If Powers was a good swordsman, Bentham was his equal.

The young man had studied more than gunnery during his residence in France.

Jupe, the darky, drew off and gazed at the duellists with distended eyes. Never before had he witnessed such a combat.

The rivals fought with much bitterness; lunge, parry, thrust and counter-thrust followed in quick succession.

Gilmor held the lantern in a manner that revealed the thrilling scene.

All at once Captain Powers' blade was twisted from his hand by a dexterous movement which he had not foreseen, and, as the weapon fell at the water's edge, he realized that he was at Bentham's mercy.

Quick as a flash his right hand flew to the belt that carried his pistols.

"Is that your game?" cried Bentham. "If it is, by Jove, I'll block it here!"

Our hero lunged straight at his rival's breast, and before an arm could be interposed the bright point of the sword had disappeared.

Captain Powers staggered back with a groan, as a figure rushed past Bentham.

It was the figure of Jupe.

With the fury of a tiger the darky threw himself upon Gilmor, whom he dealt several terrible blows in quick succession, and who fell to the ground when released.

"He war drawin' his pistol, Massa Bob, an' I thought I'd hinder 'im," said Jupe, returning to Bentham, with victory in his eyes. "I guess de coast am cl'ar now. Cap'n Powers doesn't seem to be dead, but he can't interfere any mo'. Shall we try it ag'in?"

Bentham stepped once more into the boat, but not without a glance at the two figures lying motionless on the duelling ground.

Jupe shoved the boat into the stream, and his strong black arms propelled it rapidly from the spot.

It was a dangerous journey, for the picket boats of Cape Fear River were always on the alert; but fortune favored our young hero.

The boat crept from the river's mouth at last; it breasted the surf, and glided on out to sea.

An hour later a cry of " Boat ahoy !" cut the darkness.

An answer was returned, and Robert Bentham at last stood on the deck of a Union blockader.

CHAPTER VIII.

HOW A SHIP CHANGED HANDS.

It was the morning after Robert Bentham's escape from Wilmington, and Gordon Mowbray was walking his library like a caged lion.

Suddenly a rap sounded on the door.

"Come in," said Mowbray, glancing up, but not breaking his strides.

The door opened, and a well-built man, with a bandage over one eye, entered and dropped into the chair to which he was assigned by a wave of the hand.

"That nigger of yours has a fist like a sledge hammer, and muscle to suit, colonel," he said, fixing on Mowbray his one good eye that flashed angrily. "I was about to serve on that nephew of yours a writ of forcible detention in the shape of a revolver, when Jupe sprung at me like a tiger, and the three blows he dealt, all in less than a second, felt like the falls of a trip-hammer. I saw all the stars that ever glittered in the universe, and my head this morning feels as big as a mountain."

"Tell me all about it. I have heard nothing but reports. I have been waiting for you, Gilmor. I thought you would come. Go on!"

Mowbray's crisp sentences disclosed both his impatience and ill humor.

He had thrown himself into a chair in front of his

visitor, who was Flash Gilmor, Captain Powers' second in the duel on the river bank the evening before.

"Dick and I were hunted up last night by Tom, who, somehow or other, had discovered your nephew was going to join the Yankees against us," began Gilmor. "We at once resolved to thwart him, and to clip his wing feathers at the same time. There was no intention of hurting him. The duel that was fought he brought about himself. We—Dick and myself—started for your house immediately after getting Tom's news, and on our way we saw Bentham and Jupe cross the street ahead of us, moving toward the river. Of course we followed and saw that nigger pull a boat from the water. Everything was plain, then. The two were going to the Yankee fleet, and we had a right to detain them. The captain called a halt, when Bentham jumped from the boat, opened his coat, showing that he was fully prepared for a fight, and rushed at Powers with a sword. That brought on the fight."

"Well?" said Mr. Mowbray impatiently.

"They must have fought for five minutes without one gaining any advantage over the other. If Powers knows how to handle a sword, I now know that Bob Bentham practiced fencing while abroad. At last he got in a pass and a twist that disarmed the captain, and before the lost ground could be recovered his sword transfixed the disarmed man. Then I attempted to draw my revolver, but that rascally black Jupe, rushed up and put me *hors de combat* beside Powers. After that, escape for the pair was easy, and I suppose they reached the fleet."

" No doubt of it," said Mowbray ; " but how is the captain this morning?"

" A little better, the surgeon thinks. He passed a pretty good night. Bentham's blade was well directed, but fortune turned it aside. The captain says he is going to live for vengeance in more ways than one, and I know he will. The Swiftwing was to have sailed to-day, but she will not get away now until the captain is out of danger. I wish we could have detained Bentham. I suppose he got on a high horse here."

" He was not boisterous, but deeply insulting for all," said Mowbray. " I might have prevented this affray by keeping him here by force, but I did not think he would attempt to leave Wilmington so soon. I don't care what becomes of him now. He has forfeited all right to my affection. What do the people say about me, Gilmor? You have been among them?"

" About you?" exclaimed Gilmor, amazed. " Nobody blames you for anything. Your loyalty to the South is not questioned. You are not held responsible for Bentham's acts. If the citizens could catch him, I expect he would speedily adorn a lamp-post."

" No doubt of it."

" Why, the wounding of Powers causes great excitement everywhere ! Nobody seems to have heard how Bentham saved the Foxhound, thus arming three whole regiments with new Enfield rifles."

" How so?" cried Mowbray. " I had not heard of that myself."

" It was when the Foxhound was hotly beset by the Yankee fleet last night. Powell was going to blow the ship to perdition, for he had given up all hopes of making port. Well, Bob followed him down to the cabin where the skipper had concealed the fuse connecting with a torpedo in the hold, which was more than I would have done, and forced him to give up his devilish design. There's no use in talking, colonel, that nephew of yours has grit. He'll do us great injury if his career is not speedily checked. The Yankees will recognize his worth and give him an important command. We will hear of him again. I am sure of that."

Mowbray was silent for awhile.

"I have been a fool, Gilmor—a consummate dolt!" he suddenly exclaimed. "While I was paying for Bob's naval education in France he was translating important works on gunnery for the North. He admitted as much—even boasted of it—in my house last night. Still I never suspected him of treachery to the South. It is true that his father was an ardent supporter of the old government, and if he were living to-day he would command on the quarter-deck of a Yankee cruiser; but I thought the boy had forgotten those things under my care. I feel myself disgraced in a measure. Look here," and Mowbray took from the desk at his right a paper which he held up to his visitor's gaze. "Here is Bob's commission as second officer of the privateer Swiftwing. I was going to present it to him this morning, but now I consign it to its proper place—the fire!"

As he finished, the maddened Mowbray wheeled his chair halfway round, and dexterously tossed the commission upon the live coals glowing in the grate.

It caught speedily and the two men watched it burn in silence.

" With the burning of that commission has expired
my love for my only sister's child !" said Mowbray,
whirling upon Gilmor. " He shall never darken my
door again. When I learn what vessel he serves on, I
will send to sea an avenger that shall rid the Confederacy of at least one foe. I swear to do this, Gilmor,
if it takes every dollar of my wealth !"

Mowbray's clinched hand came down heavily upon
the lid of the desk, shaking up everything on the in
side, and causing Gilmor to recoil.

" He shall be hunted continually from wave to wave
—from port to port, until the chase has ended !" continued the Southerner. " My vengeance shall be no
child's play, Gilmor ! At the end of the year there
shall not run through the veins of any Yankee officer
a drop of Mowbray blood !"

" Dick Powers will pay his respects to him, you may
be sure of that, colonel," said Gilmor. " As I shall
sail in the Swiftwing, I will be in at the death."

" Of course—of course ; but I would sooner have him
caught by a vessel owned by his uncle."

" Oh, if that is it, colonel, permit me to say that the
Swiftwing is for sale."

" For sale !" echoed Mowbray, almost leaving his
chair. " What has thrown her on the market ?"

" The financial embarrassment of her builders. She
was built by private enterprise, although her officers
were to receive regular commissions from the government. She will be sold to the government unless
purchased by private parties within the next few
days."

" I will take her, Gilmor."

" At the price wanted ?"

" What is it ?"

" One hundred and thirty thousand dollars."

" The ship is mine !"

Gilmor stared at Mowbray, who now spoke with a calmness that called forth surprise.

"Shall I notify the Swiftwing's owners of your willingness to pay their price ?" Gilmor asked, making a motion to depart.

" I'll do that myself," was the reply. " I did not think I would be able to put a hunter on his track so soon. Ah ! Gilmor, you and Powers will make the Swiftwing a veritable scourge of the seas. I have confidence in Powers. He is young, but he is nobody's fool. I don't know so much about you ; but I guess you'll do. I'll see the Messrs. Bardolph within an hour and make the purchase."

" Hadn't you better inspect the ship first ?"

" No ; I don't want to lose time. I'll go through her after the bargain has been made. She is worth the price asked ?"

" Yes."

" Your word is guarantee enough, Gilmor."

Five minutes later Flash Gilmor left the Mowbray home with triumph sparkling in his eye.

" A good morning's work," he said gleefully. " A cool twenty thousand made without much talking. I found him in the proper humor, and when I had worked him up to the right pitch, I had but to mention that the Swiftwing was for sale. He thinks I'm going in the ship, ha ! ha ! When the time comes, I'll slide out out of the affair, for if I would win in the important game I am playing I must remain in Wilmington."

Not far away Gilmor met a man who seemed to be

waiting for him. The two met cordially, and went off arm in arm like confidential friends.

" Well, she is off your hands, Bardolph !" exclaimed Gilmor.

" The devil you say," exclaimed young Mr. Bardolph. " Who is the purchaser ?"

" Gordon Mowbray."

"The deuce ! At what price ?"

" The one you named."

" Good ! Gilmor, you don't know what a load you've lifted from my heart. You shall have your commission as soon as Mowbray secures the payments. Sold ! and well sold, too."

" That's what I say."

" She'll never run the blockade, Gilmor. Those Yankee ships will redouble their vigilance since the Foxhound got in with such a valuable cargo, and the Swiftwing will either be sunk or captured within sight of the coast. Then—but you know the rest."

" Yes," said Gilmor ; and then he added under his breath. " And that's why I never intend to sail in the Swiftwing."

The two men adjourned to a neighboring wine shop, and, over the costliest vintage the proprietor could place before them, they drank to the successful sale of the new privateer, which, in Mowbray's mind, was to sweep the seas and rid him forever of his troublesome nephew.

An hour later they left the drinking-place and sought out the office of the Messrs. Bardolph, where the senior member of the firm told them that Gordon Mowbray had just departed, carrying with him certain papers which constituted him sole owner of the privateer.

Of course another season of rejoicing followed; more wine, and more mutual congratulations.

"Mowbray inquired where Powers was, and I told him. I think he went thither," said the elder Bardolph.

Yes, Mowbray had sought out the wounded captain, who had been removed to his cabin on board the Swiftwing.

He was overjoyed to see the Southerner.

"Look here," said Mowbray, depositing the deeds on his couch. "You will stand on my decks when you go to sea. I want you to do your duty: but I know you will, captain. Don't spare a Yankee ship; but above all, hunt Bob Bentham down!"

"What shall my reward be?" asked Powers, looking into Mowbray's eyes.

"Norah."

The hand of the wounded captain crept toward Mowbray and the two men grasped.

"This is a promise, colonel," asked Powers eagerly.

"I will bind it with an oath if you say so."

"No, no! The promise of a Mowbray is enough."

"You have it!"

"The Swiftwing leaves Wilmington to-morrow night."

Mowbray started.

"My wound doesn't bother me since you have spoken," said Powers, with a faint smile. "Once at sea, I shall speedily recover. I long to pay my enemy back for his devilish thrust. The Swiftwing will cut loose to-morrow night. You may depend on that, colonel."

Mowbray left the young officer and inspected the ship. Everything he saw satisfied him, but there were some things he did not see.

CHAPTER IX.

BENTHAM MEETS THE MERRIMAC.

HAVING seen Bentham, the loyal gunner, reach the blockading fleet safely, we are compelled in order to follow him to transfer the reader from Wilmington over a space of nearly two months and a long stretch of sea to the deck of a vessel lying within cannon-shot of Fortress Monroe.

This vessel is the Cumberland, a ship whose name stands proudly on the annals of time, and whom fame has transferred to a niche of glory.

For some time rumors of the building of an iron monster at Norfolk by the Confederates had daily reached the Union fleet lying off the fortress, and glasses had long been trained toward Sewall's Point, from which direction the new sweeper of the seas was expected.

This formidable foe was the rebuilt United States ship Merrimac, which had been scuttled and sunk by the government forces at the abandoning of the Norfolk Navy Yard.

The Confederates had succeeded in raising the hull of the Merrimac, and by a thorough reconstruction, rendered her one of the most powerful war vessels afloat.

To effect this they had cut her hull down to within three feet of the watermark. strengthening her by adding a sloping bombproof, which covered her gun deck with bars of railroad iron.

She had no masts; her smokestack and pilot-house were the only exposed objects above deck.

Her bows possessed a steel "ram" for piercing the enemy's ships, and fore and aft she was amply protected by a plating of steel.

The Merrimac, rechristened the "Virginia" by her new owners, carried twelve guns of the most formidable character—eleven-inch navy guns at her sides, and one-hundred pounders at the stern and bow.

Thus equipped, the Merrimac was ready to grapple with the whole Federal navy.

No wooden vessels could withstand her assaults.

Captain Buchanan, her commander, knew her strength, and was eager to test it.

We have said that Bentham was on board the Cumberland.

After reaching the blockading fleet, he went North, but soon afterward found himself at Fortress Monroe on his return, where he asked for and obtained the position of gunner on the Cumberland, in anticipation of the Merrimac's speedy appearance.

The Cumberland was a well-built sloop-of-war of 1,725 tons burden. She carried twenty-four guns—ten-inch pivots, and rifled cannon. She was considered one of the most effective wooden vessels in the navy at the time, and her acting commander, Lieutenant George W. Morris, had confidence in her abilities.

At last the much-talked-of monster made her appearance.

It was the eighth of March, and the sun was sloping westward from his meridian.

The glasses of the Union officers soon discovered her as she moved steadily by the channel in front of Sewall's Point.

The Federal batteries warned the ships blockading the mouth of the James, and everybody became on the alert.

The long-looked-for hour was at hand, and one of the most desperate of naval battles was about to take place.

Confident of her destructive powers, the ironclad ship made directly for the Cumberland and Congress. Her ports were closed, and as she came within range the Congress opened on her with her heavy guns.

As well might the Federalists have hurled handfuls of peas against the Merrimac's steel sheathing.

All at once the fire of the Congress was returned by her mailed antagonist, and the terrible shot tore mercilessly through her wooden sides.

"We are in for it now," said a young officer on board the Cumberland, as the Merrimac, after delivering her broadside at the Congress, steered for her consort. "Give her the best you have in the locker, Bentham. The progress of this ram must be stopped if possible."

"Ay, ay, sir," replied Bentham, saluting the officer as he turned away. "I have my first chance for showing the result of my study, and that beneath the flag my father once fought under."

The Merrimac continued to approach.

Bentham carefully sighted his gun, and all at once the heavy shot broke the silence that reigned on the gun-deck.

The ball struck the Merrimac, showing that it had

been well aimed, but took no effect, merely glancing upward and flying off.

Bentham, who had watched the shot, turned quietly to the officer of the division.

" We can't stop that craft, sir," he said respectfully.

The next moment the Cumberland delivered a broadside which would have sunk the largest wooden vessel afloat.

The balls struck the Merrimac in every conceivable place, but she still moved on.

Could nothing check her ?

Was she destined to gain a victory which would place the great seaboard cities of the North at her mercy ?

" Great heavens! she is going to strike us!" exclaimed Bentham, who saw the Merrimac rounding to after the broadside.

This was the Confederate's intention.

Head on, she made for the Cumberland, from whose guns belched forth a perfect rain of iron and steel.

The shock was terrible.

The steel prow, which nothing could resist, struck the Cumberland about amidships, literally laying her open, and placing her at once in a sinking condition.

Still her heroes stood by their guns.

Broadside after broadside they poured against the steel sides of their foe, while her guns continually raked them fore and aft, filling the cockpit with wounded, and making her decks slippery with blood.

It was a terrible moment.

Bentham, his face powder-burned and his clothes splashed by the blood of his comrades, fought his gun with the courage of a young lion.

"We fight as long as we float, boys!" he said to his companions. "The old flag still waves overhead. Give the Confederates some more doses of iron! Hurrah for the Union!"

Bravery would not save the day.

The Cumberland, gallant ship, was doomed!

Water was rushing into her forward magazine, and the cries of the wounded added to the horror of the scene.

Some of the guns almost touched the waves, but the Union tars still worked them, occasionally sending up loud cheers of defiance.

Braver men never fought a ship.

To add to the terrible spectacle, the after pivot gun got loose and rolled about, crushing men without mercy, and hastening the fate of the vessel.

The flag of the Cumberland continued to wave over her gallant crew. It inspired them with new courage, and called forth cheer after cheer as the grand old ship settled toward the depths of the sea.

Without pity and as destructively as ever, the Merrimac continued to deliver her terrific broadsides into the Cumberland.

The shot opened great gashes wherever they struck, and the blood of the Cumberland's tars ran through them into the sea.

At last, when destruction seemed unavoidable, the boats were ordered out.

They were brought alongside with difficulty.

The men could hardly escape from the gun-deck to the spar-deck, the ship was sinking so rapidly; they climbed into the rigging, or sprung overboard to save their lives.

"Come, Bentham," said an officer to the young gunner, who was loading one of the guns with his own hands. "We shall sink in less than five minutes."

"One more shot, sir! Here, men, let us give that devil a parting salute!"

Several sailors sprung to his side with enthusiastic cheers.

The gun was sighted by Bentham and fired.

The next moment the muzzle of the piece was under water!

It was, indeed, the last shot.

Bentham reached the rigging as the spar-deck disappeared from view beneath the seething sea.

"Jump, Bentham!" called out the young officer, and the heroic gunner who had covered himself with glory sprung as far out as possible as the vessel passed out of sight forever.

After battling with the waves for awhile, Bentham was picked up, and rowed, with others, toward the frowning fortress, from whose walls hundreds had witnessed the fight.

Scores of the Cumberland's crew went down to the depths with her, among them her chaplain, whose last words were words of comfort to the dying.

The frigate's destruction was complete; but the Merrimac was not satisfied.

She turned her prow toward the crippled Congress, and sent her resistless shot clean through her wooden sides.

But the Yankee tars fought their vessel nobly.

Their captain fell in the action; the decks grew slippery under their feet; they were in danger of sharing the Cumberland's fate.

At last the Congress made for the beach, where she grounded.

Then the heartless enemy approached, and poured broadside after broadside into her, until she hauled down her colors and surrendered.

Night was fast settling over this scene.

The darkness was lit up by the flashes of the Merrimac's guns.

She was now turning her attention to the powerful steamship Minnesota, which had grounded, and lay apparently at her mercy.

Captain Van Brunt trained his heaviest cannon on the steel-mailed monster, but the shot produced no effect.

Where would the ram's work end?

It was the gloomiest Saturday night the Union cause had yet known.

The fight between the Minnesota on one side and the Merrimac and her consorts, two steamers, on the other, lasted until seven o'clock, when the ram drew off and steamed back toward Norfolk.

The day was hers.

She had destroyed two war vessels, and left another —the Minnesota—in a precarious condition.

Everybody believed that she would return on the following day and complete her mission—the destruction of every Federal ship blockading the mouth of the James.

Then she would turn her prow northward, and Baltimore, Philadelphia and New York would hear the thunder of her guns.

It was, indeed, the most critical hour of the whole war—the second day at Gettysburg not excepted.

" They tell me," said Bentham, addressing an officer in the fortress, " that the Monitor is expected to-night."

" She should be here now, sir," was the reply ; " but she cannot turn the tide. The Merrimac is invulnerable. I fear Ericsson has toiled for nothing !"

CHAPTER X.

THE BATTLE OF THE GIANTS.

It was known by the anxious Federals that the Monitor had left New York; but what had become of her?

Had she foundered at sea, leaving the Merrimac to continue unchecked her career of devastation?

Every eye was turned toward the Cape Charles Light.

Suddenly several shouts went up from the lips of those who were provided with glasses.

A movable light was approaching!

"The Monitor! the Monitor!" passed from mouth to mouth.

Was it time that the Ericsson battery was near at hand?

As the light broadened, illumining the waters as they came on, all doubts were dispelled, and the news spread like wildfire.

At nine o'clock that eventful night the Monitor ran under the frowning guns of Fortress Monroe, and came to anchor there.

Lieutenant Worden, her commander, reported to Flag-Officer Marston and General Wool for duty, and was sent to Newport News to protect the Minnesota, whom we left aground and in a critical condition.

It was expected that on the following day the Merrimac would sally forth again to complete the destruction of the great steamship.

Night passed away, and morning came.

It was the dawn of a beautiful Sabbath day, calm and peaceful.

At half-past six three vessels were seen advancing from Craney Island.

These were the Merrimac and her consorts of the day before, the Jamestown and Yorktown.

The Monitor lay quietly in the water within pro- tecting distance of the Minnesota, whose men were ready for the conflict.

Disdaining to notice the cheese-box looking craft that threatened to engage her, the Merrimac pushed straight for the Minnesota.

Captain Van Brunt at once beat to quarters, and suddenly opened on the Confederate with his stern guns, as he signaled the Monitor to engage in the attack.

Commander Worden made for the enemy, and to the surprise of every eye-witness, laid himself right alongside, and opened with his monster cannon.

The fight—the grapple of the giants—was now fairly on.

The two iron sea-dogs were at close range, muzzle to muzzle one might say, pouring their heavy metal against each other in a constant shower that seemed entirely resistless.

Yet the shot of the Merrimac fell harmless from the sides of the Monitor's revolving turret, while Worden seemed to do his antagonist no great damage.

For nearly two hours the ships battled for the mastery with the rage of wounded lions.

The Minnesota joined in the battle, pelting the Merrimac with her heaviest shot, and adding greatly to the appalling horror of the scene.

A cloud of smoke hovered over the two iron ships— a cloud which the spectators on the walls of the fort and elsewhere were afraid to see lift, lest the lifting should reveal the Monitor at the mercy of her foe.

The pall rose at last, and the stars and stripes were seen still floating over the little ship, from whose turret the terrible guns were still belching forth great globes of iron!

Maddened at the constant firing of the Minnesota, the Merrimac turned suddenly upon her.

She rushed forward with her steel prow, for the purpose of dealing a stroke like that which had finished the Cumberland.

The Monitor saw the steamer's peril, and deliberately threw herself in the enemy's path.

Her guns were fired fast and furious into the foe.

The Merrimac reeled before the awful discharges, and then resolved to bring the combat to an end.

She turned her prow upon the Monitor, and with a full head of steam on, drove straight at her.

It was an anxious, breathless moment.

The next minute the two monsters collided!

The Merrimac's prow glided up on her adversary's sheathed deck, careening her and exposing her own hull under the iron casing, an accident most unfortunate.

Quick as a flash, the Monitor seized the opportunity thus presented, and sent a ponderous shot under the enemy's sheathing, driving her off disabled.

Still the fight went on, iron against iron, steel combating steel!

The waters roared and foamed under the boats' keels, and the near shore shook under the crash of the gigantic artillery.

Would the conflict never end?

Men wondered while they watched and stood awe-stricken on the ramparts of Fortress Monroe.

Captain Buchanan, of the Merrimac, was a man of nerve.

Had he resolved to conquer or die on the battlefield of his own choosing?

On the other hand, Commander Worden was proving himself a hero.

Two braver men had never met before in a battle on the wave.

At last the Merrimac pulled off, but sullenly, like a wolf showing his teeth, and growling.

She had given up the fight, thus acknowledging that in the Monitor she had found a superior whom she could not destroy.

A cheer went up from a thousand throats.

The Federals felt that a great victory had been gained, even if the Merrimac had not been sent to the bottom of the sea.

The guns of Sewall's Point received the Confederate ram under their protection, gunboats came to her aid, and she steamed back to Norfolk.

The Monitor steamed back to the fort, where those who had witnessed the fight had an opportunity of inspecting her.

What did they see?

An iron-covered vessel, conical in shape, one hundred and seventy-four feet long, forty-one feet wide, surmounted by a revolving turret, armed with two eleven-inch columbiads.

These were the guns that had beaten off the Merrimac.

The interior of the Monitor presented no traces of carnage to her curious inspectors.

Commander Worden had his eyes bandaged, having been injured by some small scales of iron which had been knocked loose by a ball from the Merrimac.

"No thanks to the Navy Department for this protector," said one of the Monitor's visitors, an old military officer.

"Why not, sir?" was the question instantly put up by a young man.

"Because, sir, the Monitor comes to us from the hands of private citizens. The government has been afraid to trust Ericsson's genius. Now, sir, it will be acknowledged, and before the year ends there will be a hundred Monitors afloat."

This was prophecy.

The usefulness of the formidable Merrimac seemed at an end.

She had encountered her equal on the wave, and her guns would not thunder in the ports of the great commercial cities of the North.

The glad tidings quickly flew northward.

They crossed the sea and told the foreign powers that their great warships were comparatively worthless.

A revolution had taken place in naval affairs, for one Monitor was sufficient to sink a navy.

"What do you think now?" asked a young sailor, addressing Bentham, as he emerged from the Monitor after a tour of inspection through her interior. "For my part I prefer the wooden ship where one can see the balls strike, and hear the crash of timber and the fall of spars."

"So do I," answered Bentham. "A naval fight is robbed of its excitement and dangers when the sailors are protected by iron plating which no shot can penetrate. Ay, sir, give me the wooden ship any time, and let me have charge of a gun—that is all I ask."

"Where do you serve next? Your ship, the Cumberland, will never float again."

"I'm out of a job, but not for long, I trust," smiled Bentham. "I did not leave France to idle my time away here. I am anxious for work. I am willing to serve anywhere."

Several days later the young gunner was summoned on board Commander Marston's vessel.

"We have heard of your bravery on board the Cumberland," said that officer, addressing Bentham, whose face colored as he spoke. "We understand, sir, that you desire more active service."

"That is correct, sir."

"A new vessel, called the Avenger, fitted out for the purpose of overhauling blockade runners and privateers is expected here to-morrow. Will you accept a position on her decks?"

"In what capacity?"

"As second officer."

"No, sir," said Bentham promptly, and greatly to the officer's astonishment. "I want no better than to be a gunner. I flatter myself that I know something about gunnery."

"We are all aware of that," was the smiling reply; "but the government believes that it owes you something for your helpful books and your conduct on board the ill-fated Cumberland. The place of second officer on the Avenger is at your command."

" Give me charge of a gun, and let another go to the quarter-deck."

"It shall be as you desire, sir," said Marston. " Promotion is bound to find you wherever you be. The Avenger will be here to-morrow; such are our advices at any rate."

This terminated the interview, and Bentham departed to join the friends who were waiting to congratulate him.

".A letter for you, Mr. Bentham," said a youth, joining the group with a packet which he extended toward the young gunner. " It was found under the bastions, weighted down with a stone."

Bentham took the paper, which was not inclosed in an envelope, but was simply folded, and opened it.

Those who watched him read saw his eyes light up suddenly with joy, and his cheeks flush like the cheeks of a schoolboy.

This is what Bentham read:

" Cousin Bob: I was shocked to learn of your sudden departure, but not greatly surprised at the sentiments you have openly avowed. Wherever you go do not forget that my thoughts are with you, nor that my wishes are for your success. Your Uncle Gordon has purchased and sent to sea a vessel called the Swift-wing—the one you were to have sailed in under the Confederate flag. He is very much incensed against you, and I believe he has given Captain Powers—who was in a fair way for recovery when he left—special instructions to hunt you down. I am confident, Cousin Bob, that you are quite able to take care of yourself as well as to attend to Captain Powers should you meet

him.   Flash Gilmor did not sail in the Swiftwing.   He
was sick at the time.   The Foxhound, Captain Powell,
got to sea again last night with a cargo of cotton.   It
is known here that he will again attempt to run the
blockade with a cargo of valuables for the Confederate
armies.

"I trust that you will do your whole duty, remem-
bering always that my heart is with the old flag, if
the new one does wave over Wilmington.   Affection-
ately.   NORAH."

"A love letter, by Jove!" exclaimed one of
Bentham's companions, as the gunner reached the end
of the communication.

"Not so much a love letter as a warning from a
valued friend," was the reply, as Bentham put the
letter away.

He was puzzled by the strange delivery of the letter
from the beautiful girl he left in Wilmington.

Who had carried it to the spot where it had been
found?

Why had it not been delivered directly to him?

These were questions that deepened the mystery,
and Bentham was compelled to give them up.

In the quietude of his quarters that night he read
the letter again and again.

He knew that one heart was with him in blockaded
Wilmington that night.

What cared he if all the rest were against him?

He was eager to push to sea, and awaited with impatience the coming of the Avenger.

CHAPTER XI.

" you must give him up !"

TRUE it was, as written by Norah's hand in the mysteriously delivered letter, that the privateer Swiftwing had got to sea, and true also that Flash Gilmor, who had pocketed a cool twenty thousand by the sale of the ship to Mowbray, had remained behind.

Gilmor's apparent disappointment at being left was very great.

His physician had certified to Mowbray that he was too sick to go out with the privateer, but it was a bit astonishing how suddenly his patient recovered when the Swiftwing had run the blockade.

He declared that he would proceed at once to Charleston and embark on a swift sailing vessel, with hopes of overtaking the privateer; but he soon forgot his declaration, for he loitered around Wilmington as though he considered it the safest place.

Gordon Mowbray had seen fit to give Captain Powers sealed instructions, which were not to be opened until a certain point had been reached.

"The Swiftwing is a complete vessel in every part," he said to Norah, when he returned from witnessing the privateer's departure from her moorings. "She will make sad havoc among the Yankee merchantmen. I have confidence in Powers. If he is a young man he knows how to sail and fight a ship."

Norah said nothing for a time.

She stood at the window, her shapely figure half concealed by the elegant lace curtains that touched the floor, and her eyes fixed abstractedly on the shadows of the night gathering outside.

"I have no doubt that the Swiftwing will prove formidable to her foes," she said, glancing over her shoulder at her foster father, who had thrown himself into an armchair and was gazing at her.

"What do you think of her commander, Norah?" asked Mowbray.

"A brave fellow, no doubt, and a good sailor."

"Is that all?"

The girl colored slightly.

"A handsome man, if you like, sir," she answered.

"Nothing more?"

Norah turned from the window and approached Mowbray, at whose side she suddenly stopped, and into whose upturned eyes she looked calmly.

"You are getting at something, Uncle Gordon, but I am puzzled," she said, smiling. "Come, relieve me; solve the enigma. I am all attention."

As she finished, the fair girl drew a chair up to Mowbray's side and seated herself in it with her face turned upon the Southerner.

"My words should not be a puzzle, Norah," he said. "I do not see why you see in Captain Powers only a brave fellow and a good sailor. Is that all a young lady should see in her lover?"

Nora started.

"My lover? Captain Powers a suitor for my hand?"

Mowbray seemed to enjoy her surprise.

"What else could he be?" he asked. "He has been our most frequent visitor ever since the war opened.

Of course, Norah, I once thought that you were to become my nephew's wife, but his treachery has changed all that, and you must look out for a loyal husband. Let me see. You are nineteen, girl; old enough to choose a husband. Bentham is out of the question. You do not think of him, I hope?"

The hand that touched Mowbray's arm trembled like an aspen leaf, and all color fled from its fair possessor's face.

"She thinks of him still," went through Mowbray's mind. "If I leave everything to her I will have trouble in keeping my promise with Powers. I shall open the home campaign at once. This girl shall understand that I am master here."

He kept his eyes fixed on the girl.

"I want you to banish my nephew from your mind —to tear him from your heart, if he still remains there," he said, with a Mowbray's sternness. "He is going to be hunted like a pirate by the ship I have just sent to sea. Captain Powers and I have taken mutual oaths, which shall be kept. Nay, do not start, Norah. You have lived too long under this roof to know that I have never broken a promise. Robert Bentham has covered the Mowbray ancestry with infamy. I never thought he'd do this while I encouraged his love-making. I expected to see him sail under the stars and bars, and not under the banner of the North. He came back to fight against us all—against you and I, girl. My money educated him; it taught him the art of gunnery in order that he might sink our vessels. I fly into a passion whenever I think of this. I say that you and I have seen him for the last time. Make up your mind to that, Norah. Dick Powers will do his duty!"

Norah withdrew her hand from Mowbray's arm and rose without speaking.

She was asked to give Bentham up for a man who had gone to sea to hunt him down; to throw to the winds at one time all the love that had grown and flourished in her heart through a number of happy years.

She now saw that Mowbray had promised her hand to Powers, the captain of the Swiftwing, on condition that he fulfilled his part of the bargain, a thought of which sent a cold shudder through her frame.

"Come back here, Norah," said Mowbray, as she was moving off without replying to his stern language.

She turned and faced him, pale as a lily, but with her hands clinched and lips pressed firmly together.

" I want you to do what I desire in this matter," continued Mowbray. "Promise that you will let the Yankee gunner go, and turn your attention to the nobler lover, the man who remains true to the South— Captain Powers, of the Swiftwing."

Rebellion lit up the girl's eyes.

She seemed to increase an inch in her stature.

" I make no promises," she said firmly. " I will let the future answer for itself."

Mowbray sprung up, his face flushing, and his eyes emitting flashes of rage.

" What's that? Treason in Mowbray House?" he roared, springing at the girl, whose wrist one of his hands encircled before she could fly, even if flight had been her intention. " Say those words again. No! Keep still! I will not have them uttered here again. Once is enough! You shall become the wife of Captain Powers. I have promised him your hand, and I will see that that promise is fulfilled to the letter. You shall not balk me, girl! *I* am master here. *I* reign in Mowbray House. Sooner than see you Bentham's wife I'd send you to sea in the Swiftwing with a lighted fuse at the door of her magazine !"

A cry of horror pealed from Norah's lips, and when Mowbray released her she reeled away and fell near the door insensible.

"Oh, I intend to be master here !" he exclaimed, gazing upon her figure stretched on the rich carpet. "By Jove ! I'd rather sink her in the Swiftwing than see her my nephew's wife. I meant just what I said when I told her that."

A tinkling bell in the hallway started Mowbray as he finished, and a bound carried him to Norah's side.

"My visitor can wait a moment," he said, picking the lovely form up and disappearing quickly from the room. "He rings like Gilmor—but that fellow was terribly ill when I last heard of him."

He bore Norah to her boudoir, and told a colored girl to attend to her, while he waited on his visitor in person.

The next moment Mowbray was at the door.

A muffled figure stood on the step extending a letter which Mowbray took without an invitation, and turned back into the house, eager to peruse its contents.

He had not asked the letter-carrier to enter while he read.

If he had, the invitation would not have been accepted, for the person had already disappeared.

Mowbray stood under an elegant hanging lamp as he broke the seal of the document and smoothed its **folds.**

All at once he started and uttered a wild cry.

"My soul! it cannot be! This letter is a lie!" rang from his lips. "Somebody is trying to frighten me. Men who have the cause of the South at heart would not be so heartless! Yes; this letter is an infamous lie, penned for a purpose!"

He stared wildly at the paper while these exclamations rung forth.

Two sentences met his gaze.

They were enough, for they ran thus:

"The Swiftwing is a floating death-trap! The Messrs. Bardolph and others knew it when they disposed of her!"

Mowbray stared a moment longer at these words.

"A lie! a lie! I will prove it!" he cried, rushing from the house.

He speedily found his way to the office lately occupied by the original owners of the Swiftwing.

Although the hour was early, the shutters were up, and there was a deserted look to the place.

The excited man shook the door, uttering oath after oath as his rage increased.

"Halloo! Mowbray! What's up?" inquired a voice from behind.

Mowbray desisted and turned.

"Ho! is it you, Powell?" he exclaimed, recognizing the blockade runner. "I want to see the Bardolphs. I have been told——"

He paused abruptly as if catching himself on the threshold of a secret.

"Don't stop, colonel," grinned Powell. "I think— I know what you have been told?"

"You!"

The blockade runner bowed.

"I have just discovered it myself, but I am not here for the purpose of seeing the Bardolphs. They left yesterday, baggage and all, and my opinion is that we have seen the last of them."

Mowbray seemed thunderstruck.

"What's to be done, Powell?" he gasped. "Cannot the Swiftwing be overhauled?"

"No; it is too late for that," was the reply of the Foxhound's commander. "Everything depends on her captain. Powers may discover the condition of the ship and put back! She isn't seaworthy, if what I've heard is half true. Still, she may be able to make Nassau. I have a good deal of confidence in Powers' sailing qualities, if we aren't warm personal friends. Gilmor didn't go."

"He was too sick to be moved."

The blockade runner smiled.

"Too sick, eh?" he ejaculated, and then he added, in a significant tone that attracted Mowbray: "I've known Flash Gilmor to have such spells before. He'll be up and about to-morrow cursing the sickness that kept him from sailing in the new privateer."

Mowbray could not speak.

His look was a stare.

Captain Powell did not continue, but began to move on, and soon passed out of sight. Mowbray was alone.

"The Swiftwing and her captain doomed? One hundred and thirty thousand gone to the bottom of the sea?" crossed his lips. "I wish I had a revolver at the head of the villain who projected this infamy!"

CHAPTER XII.

THE FOXHOUND PUTS TO SEA.

MOWBRAY's rage abated and he felt like a different man, when, a few days afterward, he learned of the Swiftwing's safe arrival at Nassau.

She had weathered gales and escaped the vigilant Federal cruisers, but beyond this Mowbray knew nothing.

Nobody could relate for him the terrible experiences of her captain and crew.

After all, thought the Southerner, the reports of the privateer's condition might have been exaggerations, coined by his enemies for the purpose of disturbing his peace of mind.

He was not going to believe that the ship was a shoddy affair, built to be sold in port by the Bardolphs, who left Wilmington six hours after the sale.

Flash Gilmor almost fulfilled Captain Powell's prediction that he would be out on the streets the day after the privateer's departure.

A few days afterward, his indisposition suddenly left him, and his friends—the schemer had friends—saw his face again.

The reader will recall a part of Norah's letter to young Bentham in which the girl mentioned the Foxhound's departure in the night.

It was true that Captain Powell had slipped his

cables, but a mistake, by intimation, that he had safely reached the high seas.

Norah's letter had been dispatched when she learned that Powell had been driven back by the blockading fleet.

Once more the trim blockade runner lay at the wharves, with a cursing captain on her deck and a dissatisfied crew below.

"Better luck next time. Curse the Yankee fleet!" growled Powell, looking madly toward the tall masts of the blockaders that lay beyond the bar in the broad light of another day. "One of these days, by Jove! I'll lay alongside one of their frigates and blow her out of the water. They don't want to play with Ralph Powell. They handle fire when they do."

That evening the blockade runner was visited on shipboard by Gordon Mowbray.

"When are you going to try to get out of here again?" he asked.

"To-morrow night. We'll have a gale then, or I'm no sailor."

"This will be your third attempt, I think."

"Yes. I've been here seven weeks and mean to get off now."

"Ah! What are your accommodations for passengers?"

"Not very ample, sir."

"Could you take out two?"

"That depends."

"Certainly; I understand that," said Mowbray.

"I have decided to take Norah to Nassau."

Powell looked his surprise.

"You go to Nassau, captain?"

" Yes."

" We will go with you."

" I don't like to run a young girl into danger," said Powell frankly. " The life of a blockade runner is always full of peril. You saw the legend over my cabin door as you entered ?"

" Yes, sir."

" I mean every word of it. This ship is never to be surrendered !"

The captain of the Foxhound spoke with resoluteness.

" I am willing to take the chances," answered Mowbray. " You will not have to carry your oath into effect."

" If you are going to Nassau, my only stateroom is at your disposal. I do not expect any other passengers. People are not eager to leave Wilmington just now."

The interview terminated a few minutes later, and, after Mowbray's departure, Powell ordered the stateroom got ready for the Southerner and his *protegée*.

Mowbray had several reasons for leaving Wilmington at that time. Since Bentham's open avowal of loyal sentiments and his escape, a good deal of popular indignation arose against Mowbray.

He was accused by some of his enemies of being in sympathy with the North, when the Confederacy possessed no truer friend.

He thought that a few months' absence would produce a change in the sentiments of those who suspected him ; and of course he would not leave Wilmington without taking Norah along.

Then he was anxious to get some news from the Swiftwing.

Since her reported arrival at Nassau, the great ren-
dezvous for Confederate cruisers and blockade runners,
he had not heard a word from her.

What had become of Powers?

The day after Mowbray's visit to Captain Powell,
another man came aboard the Foxhound.

He was a fine-looking individual, with a glossy black
beard, which of itself stamped him an important
personage. .

" When do you get off ?"_ he said to Powell.

" To-night."

" Without fail ?"

" Such is my expectation."

" Good ! I go with you to Nassau."

" The deuce you do !" was at the end of Powell's
tongue; but he did not let it go.   .

" I am sorry that I cannot take you, sir; but the
truth of the matter is that my two staterooms——"

" I can get along without a stateroom, captain," was
the interruption; and the speaker laughed. " I must
go to Nassau; there can be no ifs and buts about
it. I am an agent of the Confederate government,
and——"

" Beg your pardon, sir," said Powell. " You shall
go with me then in spite of a thousand Yankee blockaders. I'll make you as comfortable as possible in my
own cabin, while I will bunk with Mr. Cresson, my
second officer. Where is your luggage ?"

" I have none."

Thus the Foxhound got another passenger, and
Powell threw a quick but penetrating glance at him as
they separated.

" I've seen a man of his make-up somewhere," he

said to himself; "but just where I can't make out now. I don't remember that big beard, though; I think the man didn't have it when I knew him. By Jove! I forgot to ask him his name. Never mind, I'll steer afoul of it when I tackle him again."

The afternoon was going fast when Mowbray and Norah, accompanied by their baggage, came aboard and were greeted by Powell.

The young girl was pale and nervous, but very beautiful.

She did not seem sad at the thought of leaving the old Carolina city where all the happy years of her life had been spent.

Was she not going abroad on the trackless ocean where Bentham was winning his first laurels in the service of his country?

They might meet, and Mowbray might lose the beautiful mistress of his home.

The Foxhound was getting ready for sea, and Powell was busy with a captain's duties when Mowbray and his ward took possession of the staterooms which had been fitted up for their accommodation.

"That graceless nephew of yours occupied yonder stateroom during the passage over," smiled Powell, as he ushered his passengers into the cabin; "but your daughter will not object to it on that account, I know."

Mowbray's brow darkened as he answered with an effort:

"Of course not, captain. Norah and I are not to be troubled by the past, but pleased and benefited by the future. We will get off about——"

"About ten to-night. The wind is freshening

already, just as I expected, and by that time the
Yankee fleet will stand out to sea close-hauled, and
combating a gale. It will be our time. The Foxhound
will slip through all right, and to-morrow there'll be
some round swearing done on many a quarter-deck.
By the way, colonel, I've got another passenger."

"Ah !"

"An agent of the government."

"His name ?" asked Mowbray, starting.

"Bless me! if I know—an oversight on my part,"
laughed Powell. "He's bound for Nassau, too. Hasn't
come aboard yet, but I am expecting him every
minute."

It was evident that the information did not please
Mowbray.

Had the government set a spy at his heels ?

"I don't like this situation of affairs at all," he said
to Norah, when Powell had taken his departure.
"There'll be a scene on board this ship if I catch that
agent watching us. I'm not going to be shadowed
like a criminal because my nephew saw fit to unite
with the Yankees. I have never been watched, and,
by Jove! I never will be !"

Nine o'clock came.

The wind was already blowing great guns, and the
lights on board the Federal blockaders were mere
sparks of fire on the stormy sea.

The lookouts on the forts knew that the fleet had
been compelled to haul off to escape the dangerous
breakers.

The opportunity for the Foxhound getting out was
good. It looked as though fortune had raised the storm
to help her off.

At ten the blockade runner quietly slipped her cables, and with the stanch old pilot, Foulweather Tom, on the bridge, dropped noiselessly down the river with her narrow prow turned seaward.

It was a moment of subdued excitement.

Not a light was visible about the craft, but the pilot knew his duty, and she crept seaward like a thing of life.

"We'll make it!" said Powell to Mowbray, who stood at his side on the upper deck. "This time we'll get to sea, for it's growing thick as mud seaward."

Mowbray expressed gratification at the Foxhound's progress, but his thoughts could not keep from the blockade runner's other passenger—the Confederate agent.

"What is your other passenger's name, captain?" he suddenly asked Powell.

"Catesby—Gerald Catesby, I believe. Ever heard of him?"

"No."

"Then, of course, you've never met," continued the blockade runner. "When we get to sea I'll make you acquainted. He knows that you're on board, for he spoke of you when he came the last time. He sticks close to his cabin, for some cause or other. I haven't seen him since he shut himself in; but we'll stir him out before the voyage is over. Ah! sir, are we not going to outwit the Yankees?"

The Foxhound was rapidly approaching the mouth of Cape Fear River, and shortly afterward she was breasting the waves of the ocean itself.

Not a sound was heard on board the steamer.

She glided through the darkness apparently without effort.

It was the critical moment.

Ralph Powell stood on deck with a powerful night-glass clutched firmly in his hands.

The gale was now at its height, and great waves beat against the Foxhound, threatening her timbers.

"There's a light almost dead ahead," suddenly whispered Powell to Mowbray, who still kept at his side.

Mowbray could hardly repress an exclamation.

"A cruiser's light, captain?"

"A signal light—that's what I call it."

"Can't we avoid the vessel?"

"I'm not going to run afoul of her if I can help it, sir," was the blockade runner's reply. "There! the confounded glare has disappeared. I know what that means."

"What, captain?"

"We've been seen."

"Impossible."

"A Yankee blockader's eyes are as keen as a fox's. I've learned that by experience; but let me give the sea-spider the slip. Don't become alarmed, colonel. Remember the legend above my cabin door. ' The Foxhound will never be taken !' "

It was true that the light which had been observed ahead had disappeared, and it behooved Powell to exert his utmost strategy in order to avoid the Federal blockader which threatened him.

The captain of the Foxhound was equal to the emergency. He had not been outwitted yet; he never would be !

The blockade runner veered a point, and then kept on her course. Her engines worked noiselessly, although the furnaces were crammed with fuel, and in anticipation of a chase Powell ordered the heads of a dozen barrels of tar to be knocked in.

On—on through the gloomy night and the tempestuous sea went the Foxhound.

Would she escape?

This was the question that was uppermost in every brain.

Suddenly a flash of fire seemed to leap from the sea off the ship's starboard side, and a shot hissed as it passed over the deck doing no harm.

"How's that, sir?" smiled Powell, looking into Mowbray's pale face. "We'll soon get out of range at the rate we're going now. He can't do that again."

Another flash quickly followed the first, but the iron shot was not heard.

"What did I tell you?" laughed the blockade runner. "It takes a gull to catch the Foxhound when she tars her furnaces!"

The Federal blockader continued to deliver some shots at the Confederate craft, but they did not prove effective.

Foulweather Tom had steered the vessel beyond danger, and two hours later her furnaces were allowed to cool, for she was no longer chased.

"Your hand, captain!" exclaimed Mowbray, turning suddenly upon Powell. "You have kept your word. We have escaped!"

"Captain Powell, permit me to thank you also."

Mowbray turned upon the speaker—Catesby, the Confederate agent—and then started with astonishment.

"Catesby?" he ejaculated, under his breath. "That man is Flash Gilmor!"

CHAPTER XIII.

AN OCEAN TRAGEDY.

GORDON MOWBRAY was a man of quick temper.

He had by no means forgotten that it was Flash Gilmor who had inveigled him into taking the privateer Swiftwing at a big figure, when he must have known that the transaction was a barefaced swindle.

This man had ever been a welcome visitor at his house, had sat at his table, and was pointed in his attentions to Norah; yet he took advantage of that very friendship to play the part of a rascal.

Mowbray could not forgive such an exhibition of double dealing.

It went against his grain and he longed to resent it.

Therefore the discovery that Flash Gilmor was on board the Foxhound, in disguise and under an alias, could not fail to disturb the wealthy Southerner.

What was this man's object in taking passage on the Foxhound?"

Nothing good at any rate, Mowbray was constrained to think.

Unable to control his feelings, and fearful of making a scene on deck, the father of Norah turned on his heel and walked away.

The girl was in her stateroom, and thither her foster-father went.

He knocked and she opened the door.

" I was afraid you had retired, my child," he said,

with some agitation. "It is past midnight. We have escaped the gunboats, and may now reasonably expect to reach Nassau, unless overhauled off Great Abaco light by a cruiser on that station.

"You look worried, papa," Norah said, noticing his lack of composure.

"I am a bit excited," he said. "Do you know who is on board the Foxhound?"

"I don't quite understand you," she answered, as the question was a puzzling one.

"You heard Captain Powell say that he had given passage to an agent of the Confederate government."

"Yes, papa."

"I have seen him. I recognized his voice immediately. That man is Flash Gilmor in disguise."

Norah started.

"It was with difficulty I kept myself from unmasking him on the spot. A man who will play his friend such a dishonest trick as Gilmor has worked on me is in my opinion a scoundrel. I am done with him forever."

"I never liked him, papa."

"I should hope not, Norah. I believe he paid you some attention, did he not?"

"Which I discouraged, papa."

"Quite right. I don't believe he is a Confederate agent at all. Were such truly the case there would be no occasion for disguise."

"Perhaps he knew we were going in the vessel, and was afraid to appear openly on account of the transaction you speak of."

"Well, there is some reason in that. I should not blame him for wishing to shirk a meeting with the man he had wronged. I did not look at it in that light. Still it runs in my mind that he is aboard this steamer for some sinister purpose, and I mean to watch and, if necessary, expose him."

"I wouldn't precipitate matters, papa, for I believe he is a desperate man when aroused."

"What makes you think so, Norah?"

"I will tell you, though I intended to keep the matter from you for peace sake."

"What do you mean? Did the villain ever insult you?" cried Mowbray, growing white with anger.

"The day you purchased the Swiftwing, Mr. Gilmor called at the house and asked for me. He was very pleasant, as he can be when he wishes to appear to the best advantage. Our interview lasted some time, and finally he made a declaration of love and asked me to be his wife."

"His wife!" ejaculated Mowbray, "the scoundrel!"

"I was surprised--unpleasantly so."

"Of course you were—you refused him."

"I did."

"Well?"

"Let us stop there."

"No, Norah; I must have it all."

"Well, he flew into a passion, and his language was such that I had to request him to leave the house."

"You acted with admirable decision."

"He gave me a look of concentrated rage, and said that I should be his wife whether I chose or not."

"The scoundrel!" grated Mowbray.

"I told him I was not afraid of any such contingency, since, as he had conducted himself in a manner unbecoming a gentleman, I should never recognize him again. He told me that I should not escape him as easy as that, and with a menacing look departed. I have not seen him since.''

" I believe this statement of yours explains his present maneuvers. I have no doubt now that he is following you to Nassau, where he expects to continue his persecution, and perhaps devise means to carry out some vile plot against you. Be on your guard against this man. I fancy Captain Powell owes him no good will. I will sound him on the subject. Between us I guess we'll make Flash Gilmor wish he had never started on this trip. I will see Powell at once. I could not sleep as the matter now stands."

"Now, papa, promise me you will do nothing rash," said Norah rather apprehensively.

But Mowbray would make no promise, and his foster-daughter watched his departure with much anxiety.

The motion of the steamer had greatly increased, but the Southerner and his daughter had long been accustomed to trips on rough water, so they were not unpleasantly affected.

Two bells was struck on the forecastle when Mowbray attempted to mount the companion ladder just forward of the wheel, presuming that as the Foxhound seemed to be steaming through a very heavy gale that Captain Powell was probably on deck.

The storm was thundering through the rigging with an almost stunning voice, driving the fine spray wildly along, and blowing with an intensity that threatened to sweep one overboard.

The helmsman, wrapped in a thick overcoat, bent over the wheel, like a statue half seen in the mist.

As the night was bitterly cold the fine spray cut to the marrow.

As Mowbray poked his head above the protecting sides of the staircase a blast of wind nearly took his breath away.

As far as his eye could see, on every hand around, the sea, flattened until it was nearly as level as a plain, was a mass of driving foam.

The binnacle lamp burned faint and dim, with a sickly halo.

Above, however, all was clear, except a few white, fleecy clouds, driven wildly across the frosty stars that twinkled in the heavens.

The steamer heeled away to the leeward, and the heavy black smoke poured from the funnels flattened out and was swept quickly over the starboard rail.

Looking astern, Mowbray saw the billows howling after the Foxhound, urging on their white crests in fearful proximity, and threatening at every surge to roll in over the taffrail.

They looked for all the world like a pack of famished wolves, racing each other in the pursuit of the blockade runner, pitching and yelling after their prey.

Mowbray was timid of venturing upon deck, which assumed alternate slants of nearly forty degrees, and as he couldn't make out Powell through the mist, he returned to the cabin.

The swinging lamp burned low and dim.

The place was quite deserted.

"I can't do anything to-night," he muttered. "Never mind, I'll unmask him in the morning. He has further insulted me when he asked Norah for her hand. She is to become Captain Powers' wife. That has been settled, and no one shall interfere."

He carefully made his way to his own stateroom, and in half an hour was asleep, little reckoning that it was his last night of life.

In the meanwhile the Foxhound was dashing toward Nassau, as though eager to reach her destination.

Captain Powell had gone below, and Mr. Cresson, the second officer, kept watch on deck with Foul-weather Tom.

They were both on the steamer's bridge, keeping a sharp lookout forward for any signal from the man stationed at the forecastle head.

At four bells the mist lifted a bit, and suddenly the figure of the lookout was seen to wave his arm wildly, with a hoarse cry of " Port—hard a-port!" thrown by the wind violently into the pilot's teeth.

The helmsman caught the repeated order and jammed the wheel over hard.

"A brig close under our forefoot!" came the cry again from the catheads.

Mr. Cresson sprang to the starboard rail, where for a moment he was lost in a cloud of hissing spray, as the steamer careened that way.

He caught a glance of the stern of a trim-looking craft, evidently lying to in the gale.

The mist had heretofore concealed her position, and now the steamer was upon her and her fate was sealed.

Those on board the brig had only just discovered their danger.

Her helm was shifted, and there was great confusion on her deck, but it was too late to avoid the calamity.

Her sheets were let fly, and with a wild lurch she rolled over, broadside to the Foxhound, which at that instant gave a leap like a horse clearing a gate, and then——

Crash !

The blockade runner shivered with the shock from end to end, and then she flew onward, burying her nose in the sea, from which, above the shriek of the wind, came wild cries for help.

Then the ill-fated brig was whirled away astern, rolling frightfully, her masts gone by the board, and half-buried in the brine.

Foulweather Tom stopped the engines, orders were issued in quick succession, and then under low headway the steamer came about, and was headed back toward the sinking craft.

She was made out lying a short distance on the weather bow, and fast settling in the water.

The crew were seen working the pumps, while jets of brine spurted from the scuppers.

"They are sinking," said the officer of the deck to Foulweather Tom.

"Ay, ay ; God help them, for we can't. No boat will live in this sea."

"Terrible—terrible !" exclaimed Mr. Cresson sorrowfully.

Every man held his breath and looked in the direction of the brig, fearful less the next surge would submerge her forever.

The Foxhound drew as close to the sinking craft as she dared.

Several life-preservers were cast overboard attached to long lines and allowed to sweep down toward the brig.

But before anything could be done the mist settled again over the face of the sea, blotting out the unhappy vessel.

Then the Foxhound's whistle was kept going, and she lay to for a full hour, everybody hoping against hope.

Then the mist thinned again, and the water for a mile round came into view; but there was no sign of the brig within that circle.

Only the empty life-preservers tugging away at the taut lines.

The tragedy was over.

The brig had gone down with all on board.

Then Mr. Cresson sadly gave the order that put the Foxhound once more steaming on her course toward Nassau.

CHAPTER XIV.

ANOTHER TRAGEDY.

THE sun rose next morning over a troubled sea.

The gale had nearly gone down, and the sky was clear and without a cloud, but the waves still ran high, heaving their snowy crests all about the Foxhound.

The day promised to be a charming one.

When the steward summoned the occupants of the cabin to breakfast, Miss Nora Mowbray made her appearance, looking very pale, but withal very charming.

The counterfeit Catesby was already at the table, seated next to Mr. Cresson.

Captain Powell was at the head of the board, and he gallantly rose to assist Norah to her seat, which was next his own, and nearly opposite the presumed Confederate agent.

At that moment Gordon Mowbray came out of his stateroom and sat beside his daughter, not deigning to notice the man he knew to be Flash Gilmor.

The leading topic was the tragedy of the unfortunate bark, graphically described by Mr. Cresson, and the girl was horrified at the awful loss of life on board the ill-fated vessel.

After breakfast Powell invited Norah on deck.

Mowbray hovered near them, waiting for a chance to talk confidentially to the captain about the disguised passenger.

Catesby amused himself by conversing with the officer in charge of the deck.

Suddenly the lookout aloft sung out :

"Sail ho!"

"Where away?" returned Mr. Egan, the first officer.

"On the starboard bow."

"What does he look like?" said Powell, leaving Norah at the rail and joining the officer of the watch, who had sprung into the rigging and was leveling his glass at the distant craft.

"I should say it was one of Uncle Sam's sailing frigates," returned Mr. Egan ; "but he's too far off to make certain of it."

There is always some excitement and speculation at sea when a distant sail is sighted ; but of course in war times, when the stranger is more than likely to prove an enemy, this sensation is much magnified.

Half an hour later, during which the course of the Foxhound had not been changed, the vessel was easily visible from the deck.

Powell remarked to Norah that she was undoubtedly a war vessel, and was heading across the Foxhound's bows.

This made the course of each an acute angle, and necessarily they were drawing nearer each moment.

Powell was not at all uneasy, for he knew he could easily run away from the craft ahead.

During the next thirty minutes the stranger had considerably increased upon the horizon, and it was seen that he had reduced sail.

Of course the stranger's purpose was evident, but Powell gave no order to the helmsman.

He sent word to the engine-room, however, to get up a full head of steam.

At this juncture the lookout announced that a steamer was made out on the port bow.

Her hull was below the horizon as yet, but the sailor's sharp eyes had readily distinguished the telltale film of smoke.

She was heading for the frigate.

"This is growing interesting," remarked the skipper of the Foxhound.

"Are we in any danger?" inquired Norah.

"Not at present, Miss Mowbray," he replied.

"Yonder ship is an enemy, is she not?"

"Yes; a heavy sailing frigate, belonging to the United States navy. Take this glass and you will make her out quite plainly."

The focus was adjusted to suit Miss Norah.

"I see her very clearly. A perfect beauty she is," said Norah. And her heart gave a joyous throb when she recognized the Stars and Stripes floating in the breeze from her gaff.

"But we are heading straight for her, Captain Powell. Are you not afraid to meet her?"

"We shall not meet her," said Powell. "We can easily outsail her. The steamer way down under the horizon yonder, where you see the smoke, is more to be feared, if she prove an enemy. However, I am not very anxious, for the Foxhound can reel off seventeen knots in an emergency, and that's more than any Yankee craft I know of can do under forced draft."

"But why are you running toward this vessel if you really intend to avoid her?" inquired Norah, who was quite innocent of the dodges practiced by blockade runners at sea to avoid an enemy.

"Well, Miss Mowbray, I have a purpose in view. I

don't wish to lose any time getting into Nassau, and
the closer I get to yonder craft, as things stand, the
less of a detour I will have to make in order to avoid
her guns and eventually to outstrip her."

"I see," she said, with a smile. "How far off is she
now?"

"About five miles."

"I wouldn't think it, captain."

"Oh, distances are very deceptive at sea."

The frigate was heeled over under the breeze, and
made a beautiful picture in the sun, which flashed
prismatic rays from her copper sheathing along the
water.

She was reduced to easy sail, but Powell saw that
her canvas hung in such a way that within two minutes she could have all sails spread, even to her kites,
such is the rapidity and precision on board a man-of-
war.

"I'll wager that fellow is dragging a sail astern of
him to retard his speed," said Officer Egan, coming up,
glass in hand.

"An old trick, Mr. Egan," responded Powell. "But
it won't do him any good. The wind is dropping, I
believe"

"Yes, sir."

"Alter our course about half a point. That will be
enough for the present. We need only keep out of
range of his guns, you know. They have easily recognized our character by this time. How mad they'll
all be to see a rich prize escape them so easily! I
guess she is a new vessel on the Bahama station; though
what good she can do without steam beats me. She
probably carries a heavy battery, but I fancy no stea

vessel is going to come within range simply to test the matter."

The slight change in the Foxhound's course was evidently noted by the frigate's people; but they could not but be aware that a chase was out of the question, as some of their sails were even then shaking for lack of sufficient wind.

At last the frigate fired a gun forward and hoisted a signal.

The Foxhound so far showed no colors, but as this was an invitation to do so, Powell ordered the ensign of England to be run up.

As a matter of course, the Yankee cruiser placed no credence on this indication of nationality, since every blockade runner was accustomed to show the British flag.

The Foxhound altered her course a full point now, and as soon as the cruiser perceived the change her long pivot gun on the forecastle discharged an iron messenger which struck the water a cable's length short of the steamer.

Powell laughed gleefully.

" Go ahead full speed," he said to Foulweather Tom, "and keep your eye lifting for that steamer off yonder."

" Ay, ay !" said the veteran pilot.

" I believe the frigate has run up a signal for her instruction as soon as she can make it out. That, of course, can mean only one thing—a chase to head us off. There goes another gun from the Yankee," as a flash came from the Long Tom again, and another shot fell short of the Foxhound.

" Let the old gal rip !" Powell shouted to Tom on the bridge.

The Foxhound now churned the green water up under her forefoot, and darted along like her namesake.

The pseudo Catesby had retired to his stateroom for some purpose, and Mowbray, despairing of catching Powell's ear, and too impatient to cool his rising anger, determined to follow him, and have an immediate understanding.

It was an impolitic move, but the Southerner was in no mood for sober reflection.

He descended the companion-way, leaving his daughter standing by the rail, where she was too much engrossed with what promised to be an exciting issue to observe her foster-father's retirement.

When Mowbray reached the presumed Confederate agent's stateroom he knocked loudly.

The door was opened by the occupant, who, recognizing the Southerner and perceiving his mental condition, immediately understood that his disguise had been penetrated by the merchant.

For a moment the two men faced each other like a pair of duellists about to cross swords, then Mowbray, without waiting for an invitation stepped into the room.

Gilmor, alias Catesby, calmly closed the door, and without a word awaited developments.

"I have come here to unmask an imposter," said Mowbray, his voice trembling with anger. "Discard your beard, Flash Gilmor, and appear in your true colors, sir !"

The man smiled sardonically, which only increased Mowbray's rage.

"Then I will do so myself," he said, and before the

other could resent the action, the merchant made a step forward, and with a quick movement of his hand tore the disguise from the face of the Confederate agent.

Flash Gilmor stood revealed, though he still wore the flaxen wig which had completed his metamorphosis.

" Well," remarked Gilmor coolly," " you have a strange way of assaulting a man, I must say. If I choose to assume a disguise in the interest of the business I am engaged in, which is a government matter and strictly confidential, I see no reason why you should interfere."

" Flash Gilmor, I don't believe you are on a government mission at all. I believe you are working some devilment of your own hatching!"

" Indeed, sir," replied Flash, with an evil smile, " what authority have you for such an assertion?"

" That is my business, sir. I have ceased to consider you in any other light than an unprincipled scoundrel."

Gilmor smiled ironically.

" You leagued yourself with Bardolph Bros. for the purpose of defrauding me out of a large sum of money —inducing me to purchase a vessel at an exorbitant figure that you well knew was not worth half of the money. You see I know all about that transaction, sir."

Gilmor said nothing to defend himself.

" Not satisfied to enjoy the price of your infamy you have taken passage on this vessel for the purpose of still further working out your designs upon me and mine."

Flash was still silent, but his features wore the same

evil smile, and it goaded Mowbray to the pitch of madness.

"I'm not going to stop here!" he thundered. "Captain Powell shall know who his passenger really is. I don't believe there is any great love lost between you, and I am satisfied you fear him."

Gilmor received this information with a contemptuous curl of his lips, but a devilish light flashed in his eyes, and boded no good for his visitor.

"A pretty Confederate agent you are! The South wouldn't trust her interests in the hands of such a man as you."

"Are you through?" said Flash at last.

"No! My daughter has told me that you dared to ask her to be your wife. After robbing me, sir, you had the assurance to go to my house, and seek an interview with my child. You, sir, whose touch is contamination! Why, I'd sooner have her at the bottom of the sea than see her in your arms. I'd even give her to Bob Bentham sooner than to let you touch her! I want to tell you that Gordon Mowbray hates you with all the hatred that a bitter contempt and loathing engenders! I dare you to carry out the oath that fell from your lips in Norah's presence! Follow her after we have arrived at Nassau, or speak to her here on the vessel, and I will not hesitate to take such means as will rid the earth of your presence!"

There was a pause.

"Mr. Mowbray," said Flash Gilmor, with an ugly look, "you have addressed me as no man ever dared before. I have listened to you with patience because you are the father of Norah, whom I *intend* to marry in good time."

" You scoundrel! Do you——"

"Softly—you excite yourself to no purpose. You do not know me—else you would have paused before seeking this interview with the words you have uttered upon your tongue. I would *kill* any other man for less than that. Now, mark me! I have determined on making Norah my wife! I will move heaven and hell to accomplish my purpose! Such being the case, you will do well to think before thwarting me. Expose me to Captain Powell, if you dare !"

A murderous look blazed in the speaker's eyes as he uttered those words.

" I accept the challenge," said Mowbray, white with rage. " In less than five minutes he shall know that Gerald Catesby and Flash Gilmor are one and the same person."

" You mean that ?" said Flash.

" I do, as you will see," was the stern rejoiner.

" The words shall never be spoken," said Gilmor.

" And who will prevent me ?"

"I will."

The two men glared at one another an instant.

" Remember," said Gilmor, in a concentrated tone, " I have warned you. You leave this stateroom only when you have promised to be silent—as silent as the grave."

"I scorn your warning! I despise your threat! I refuse to make any promise—indeed, I reiterate what I said before : Captain Powell shall know you as you are—Flash Gilmor !"

" You are simply mad, Mr. Mowbray. I have toyed with your senile reflections and innuendoes long enough. There is a limit even to my patience. Now, sir, if you will not listen to reason, I will compel you to obedience."

Gilmor drew a revolver and placed his back against the door.

Mowbray sprang upon him like a tiger, and struck him a hard blow in the face.

" You villain " he said furiously.

" Your blood on your own head !" said Gilmor, crimson with anger, as he pushed the old man away and fired.

His victim fell without a groan.

CHAPTER XV.

CLEARED FOR ACTION.

WE must not lose sight of Robert Bentham, whom we left at Fortress Monroe awaiting the arrival of the new screw cruiser, Avenger, to which he had been appointed chief gunner.

This vessel had been built by the government expressly for the purpose of paying close attention to the Confederate privateers, many of whom had escaped to sea and were working sad havoc among the merchant marine of the country.

To be sure, most of these pests were small, chiefly fast schooners and barks, armed with a single gun as a rule, but which was as effective as a broadside when threatening an unarmed vessel; but there were also several iron steamers, commissioned by the Confederate authorities, well armed and equipped to resist even armed intervention, such for example as the Sumter and the Shenandoah, whose depredations were giving the national authorities much concern.

It was against steamers of this class that the Avenger was designed to operate.

She was a strongly built vessel, capable of a speed estimated at fifteen knots, well armed with Parrott guns of heavy caliber, including a long rifled gun amidships, which had a great reach, and was manned by a fine crew of blue jackets.

It was an open secret that many foreign governments clandestinely opened their ports to the Confederate cruisers for the purpose of coaling and revictualling.

This of course was against international law, and could only be done "under the rose."

But it showed an undercurrent of hostile sentiment against the United States, and an avowed sympathy for the Southern cause, that rendered the suppression of these scourges a hard and delicate task.

Two days after the event narrated in the preceding chapter, a vessel of war, flying the Union Jack forward and the Stars and Stripes at her gaff, was steaming slowly along some leagues east of Great Abaco light, which stood at the entrance of the northeast passage leading to the British port of Nassau.

The sun was setting in all the glory of a calm sea, gilding a burnished pathway across the wavelets, and twilight was fast settling over the face of the deep.

The captain of the cruiser was slowly pacing the weather side of his quarter-deck, absorbed in reflection.

The officer of the watch, who happened to be Mr. Haskins, the first lieutenant, was marching up and down the lee side, with his trumpet under his arm.

A couple of midshipmen, drafted from the first class of the Naval Academy at Newport, for that institution had for politic reasons been transferred from Annapolis to Rhode Island, were leaning over the lee rail in quiet conversation.

In the waist of the vessel and leaning against the long rifled Parrott pivot gun, were two men. One was our hero, Robert Bentham, the other a warrant officer, below him in rank.

"We are here, then, on the lookout for the steamer

Swiftwing, which has been refitting at Nassau ?" said the petty officer.

" Yes, that is Captain Graham's instructions. She is liable to come out at any time. Oh! I wish she'd make her appearance this evening. I think the Avenger would give a good account of herself."

" No doubt about it," replied the other, with enthusiasm.

" I am extremely desirous of trying conclusions with this vessel, for more reasons than one," said Bentham.

" Ah !"

" I know her captain, Dick Powers. He and I had a personal encounter in the suburbs of Wilmington some two months ago, and I left him half-dead on the sand."

" Indeed."

Bentham proceeded to relate to his companion the incidents attending his night escape to the Union fleet along with the negro Jupe, as already detailed in an early chapter.

Jupe, by the bye, was on board the Avenger, and was one of the crew attached to the long Parrott gun of which Chief Gunner Bentham had charge.

" I mean to give Captain Powers a specimen of my marksmanship. I should be glad if he knew I am aboard of this cruiser."

" He'll know it as soon as he shall have been brought aboard a prisoner of war," said the officer.

" And it will be gall and wormwood to his soul to meet me face to face again under such humiliating circumstances."

" It's the fortune of war."

"I should not care to have the situation reversed though ; for I do not think he would hesitate to hang me out of pure revenge for his personal defeat at my hands."

"I should hope he wouldn't go as far as that."

"There's no telling what he would do. I fancy he's a vindictive fellow, and no doubt would hunger for my blood in order to wipe out his sense of disgrace. At any rate I wouldn't care to trust him."

"There's no fear of that. The Avenger will knock the Swiftwing into a cocked hat."

"From what little I know of Dick Powers I believe he's a fire-eater, and a foe worthy of our metal."

"All the better say I."

"At any rate, the Swiftwing, if we sight her, will never go on her cruise of depredation against our merchantmen. I warrant you that," said the young gunner decisively.

"I'm sure of it," agreed the other. "By the way, I think you were a passenger on the famous blockade runner Foxhound ?"

"Yes."

"They say her captain has sworn never to be taken."

"That is quite true."

"You really believe, then, that he would blow up the vessel if hard pressed ?"

"I have not the least doubt of it."

"What a desperate man he must be !"

"The prince of reckless fellows."

"Should we get on his track we will save him the trouble of blowing up his ship. By Jove! we'll do that job for him, Bentham !"

At that moment, and before our hero could reply, the cry of "Steamer ho!" came down from the foretop watch.

"Where away?" cried the officer of the deck.

. "Two points off the starboard quarter—about five miles away."

It was too dark to make the stranger out clearly, but he showed the usual lights.

"How is he heading?"

"This way, sir."

Captain Graham sprang into the netting and leveled his night-glass at the distant steamer.

"I'll wager she's either a blockade runner or the craft I'm looking for—the Swiftwing."

Than Graham there were few better officers in the United States navy.

Although a young man, he had seen a good deal of service in different parts of the world, and had been selected to command the Avenger on account of his excellent seamanship and redoubtable courage.

He remained in the rigging several minutes examining the approaching vessel.

"Ah, here's the moon," he said, as the eastern horizon began to lighten up. "She is in her full, and we shall have plenty of light soon. You're an early riser, old girl, and I'm exceedingly obliged to you," apostrophizing the luminary, which was yet below the water line.

The Avenger bore down on the stranger, and by the time Luna had poked her shining face into view the distance between the two steamers was greatly lessened.

Whatever her character, she showed no disposition to veer off to avoid a meeting.

Therefore it was settled that she could not be a blockade runner, and must either be a British mail steamer from Nassau or the much-expected Swiftwing, presumably the latter.

A few minutes later the Avenger was prepared for action, and subdued excitement pervaded the decks fore and aft.

CHAPTER XVI.

THE AVENGER'S FIRST VICTORY.

WHATEVER wind there had been seemed to have gone down with the sun, and for the last hour the only motion in the air was what was made by the Avenger herself as she steamed along.

The moon rose on a perfectly placid sea, and the marine spectacle, as the two craft approached each other, was beautiful in the extreme.

It was a grand tropical night, and the sky, with scarcely a fleecy cloud in sight, was brilliant with stars.

A deep silence reigned about, broken only by the throb of the cruiser's engines, which was presently supplemented by a similar vibration, very light at first, from the oncoming vessel.

She was within a mile now and her character was established in the night-glass.

A two-masted bark-rigged steamer, long and low in the water, the moonlight glancing from the tube of a piece of ordnance on her forecastle.

Her side battery was not visible, the oblong ports of both vessels being closed.

A Confederate ensign floated lazily from her gaff in rabid defiance of the Yankee cruiser, while a short white pennant hung from the truck of her fore-top-mast.

The Avenger's guns were loaded and ready to be

run out at the word of command, the crew of each gun standing as silent as statues beside their piece, the captain of each cannon standing in position with drawn sword.

That was the aspect of the main gun-deck.

Above, in the waist of the cruiser, the formidable Parrott rifle pointed his long nose menacingly over the bulwark at right angle with the bowsprit; but as it worked on a pivot, its range could be shifted at will.

The vessels had drawn within a mile of each other, when a movement was noticed on the stranger's forecastle.

In a minute there was a flash of light, followed by a puff of white smoke, and as the report reached the cruiser, a heavy conical shot whizzed across her forecastle.

The fellow evidently meant business and no mistake.

Captain Graham paced the deck but made no sign.

Bentham patted the breach of his gun to allay the excitement that was coursing through his blood, swinging the weapon little by little as the line of range varied each moment.

The captain paused a moment over the break of the poop, and looked down on his chief gunner.

"Not yet, Bentham," he said calmly. "She comes on with the pride of a conqueror. We'll check her by and by. Wait till she places herself fairly at 'Old Abe's' mercy."

"Old Abe" was the name of the huge gun by which Bentham stood.

As Captain Graham had said, the steamer was

steadily approaching, apparently confident of overcoming the antagonist calmly waiting for her, for the cruiser had shut off steam and presented her broadside to the enemy.

She fired another shot, which passed diagonally across the Avenger's deck, breaking the taffrail and grazing the smokestack's steel netting, capable of turning heavy shot.

"Those fellows are no slouches with that fok's'l gun," remarked the commander.

A third shot tore up the water under the cruiser's forefoot, and across the surface of the sea to the windward.

The decisive moment had arrived.

"Now!" suddenly cried Graham to the waiting gunner. "Let her have our compliments, Bentham. Fortune speed the shot!"

A moment later the Avenger's first gun answered the privateer's defiance, and an exclamation of satisfaction fell from Bentham's lips.

He had aimed the gun himself, and had watched the shot with a night-glass.

"A gallant shot!" cried Graham. "The Swiftwing now knows what we can do. She was fairly struck. I'll wager my commission that she carries a cannon-shot in her hull at this moment, put there by Union powder. She fairly reeled under the shock. I saw this plainly."

"Good! that shot was my compliments to you, Dick Powers," murmured Bob Bentham, pleased beyond measure by Graham's words. "Now, my lads," to the crew on the gun-deck, "let us send that privateer to the bottom before she gets a chance at our merchantmen."

A cheer was the reply.

The privateer opened all her ports and immediately sent a broadside into the Avenger in answer to the shot delivered by Bentham.

"Heavens! she carries good guns," exclaimed Graham, as the vessel quivered under the iron missiles that struck her in several places. "But we have cannon just as good. One of us must be at the bottom of the sea when the fight ends.

"Ay, ay," said Bentham under his breath. "But it shall not be the Avenger!"

The moon rode serenely in the sky and cast her soft light upon the two opposing craft.

It was a moment of breathless suspense.

The Avenger had fired but one shot thus far—the one from her pivot gun directed by Bob Bentham.

The frowning muzzles of her broadside tier were run out, and the men holding the lanyards in their hands only awaited the word to fire.

The suspense was of short duration.

The Yankee vessel was on the privateer's quarter, and Captain Graham gave the order.

Like a volcano in its might sped that awful broadside on its errand, and the Avenger was enveloped in dense white smoke, which for several moments precluded the possibility of the Yankee captain ascertaining what damage his shot had done.

When it blew away to the windward the enemy was seen to be badly cut up about the hull and rigging.

Her smokestack was in ruins and the foremast was tottering.

A cheer went up from the blue jackets.

The Swiftwing—her name was easily made out

emblazoned on a flag flying from the trembling fore-topmast—answered with another well-directed broadside.

For fifteen minutes there was no intermission in the fire on both sides.

The combat was terrific.

The Confederate steamer had approached within easy gunshot of the Avenger, and the rapidity of her fire, and its destructiveness, showed that her guns were well handled.

The national cruiser's decks were repeatedly swept by her discharges, and many of the best blue jackets were sent to the cockpit, while the dead was strewn about near the guns they had so gallantly worked.

Captain Graham was manifestly surprised with the aggressiveness of his foe.

Like all naval officers he held a privateer in more or less contempt, and had calculated on an easy victory.

His own fire had been well directed, for the enemy was reduced almost to a wreck, only one mast standing, and her hull cut up in a terrible manner, yet her guns continued to work havoc.

"By George!" exclaimed Bentham, "Powers has more grit than I credited him with."

Crash!

A twenty-four pound shot smashed the bulwark nearly in front of the young gunner, and a huge splinter struck the gun with terrible force, filling the immediate air with a cloud of fractured particles.

Three of the gun's crew were badly hurt and carried below, compelling Bentham to call for volunteers to assist him.

Smash!

A heavy shot from the Swiftwing's pivot gun struck the keel of the mainmast diagonally and tore across the deck into the sea.

It was getting decidedly hot in Bentham's locality.

The enemy were evidently seeking to disable the huge gun which was working them such vital injury.

Then the Avenger shook under the broadside she delivered at that moment, and which worked destruction to the privateer, silencing many of her guns.

A minute later Bentham, after a careful aim, discharged his piece, and the shot struck the Swiftwing below the water line.

At that fateful moment an officer approached Captain Graham.

"A steamer off our starboard bow, sir."

"What colors does she fly?" answered the Yankee commander, wheeling upon the speaker.

"British, I think."

"That's only a bluff, I'll swear. How far off is she?"

"About three miles."

"Very good. When I sink this privateer I'll give her my attention."

Bentham's last shot had settled the fate of the Swiftwing, as Captain Graham presently ascertained.

"Has she struck her flag?" he inquired.

"No," returned his first lieutenant. "Her Confederate ensign is still floating from the stump of the foremast."

"Seems to me she has ceased firing."

"Our last broadside silenced her. She is a mere wreck and sinking at that."

"Bear down on her, then, Mr. Haskins; have the guns

double shotted. I'll blow her out of water if another shot is fired at us."

The Swiftwing having had her rudder shot away was now unmanageable, and the cruiser had no difficulty in taking up a raking position where a broadside would have swept her decks from stem to stern.

That would only have been a cruel act, however, for the privateer was now *hors de combat.*

The remnants of her crew were seen clambering over her lee bulwarks into the boats alongside.

She was being abandoned.

Captain Graham ordered his boats out to take possession of the prize.

In the first were sent the ship's carpenter and assistants to investigate the sinking vessel, which was slowly setting in the water.

If it were possible to save her Captain Graham meant to do so, as that meant prize money for the victors; but the prospect was not encouraging.

The second boat carried Bob Bentham, whose last shot had been so effective.

He sprang on board the Swiftwing at the head of a dozen blue jackets, and laid his hand upon the shoulder of a wounded privateersman who was trying painfully to get over the side into one of the boats.

"Where's Captain Dick Powers—he commanded this vessel, didn't he?"

"I don't know where he is," replied the man, sullenly. "He was reported dead after that last broadside from your vessel."

Bentham uttered an exclamation of disappointment.

He ran to the quarter-deck.

There were several bodies there, but none that resembled the Confederate captain.

Then he entered the cabin, which was in ruins, but without result.

Finally he descended to the cockpit, from which the wounded were being rapidly removed by the Yankee tars, and made inquiries; but no one could throw any light upon the late commander of the Swiftwing.

"I shan't believe him dead until I actually see his corpse. I'll wager he's off in one of the boats. However, we'll overhaul them all, and I shall have the pleasure of seeing my enemy face to face again."

But Bob Bentham counted his chickens too soon.

CHAPTER XVII.

THE CHASE AND THE ESCAPE.

It was the Avenger's first victory over an armed foe ; but it had been dearly purchased, for a third of her crew had been put out of action, and her hull and spars and rigging were a sight to witness.

Her smokestack escaped injury, partly because it shut up like a telescope, and during the late action was scarcely visible above the bulwarks.

One board the privateer the carpenter had reported to the officer in charge that there were several feet of water in the hold, and that it was not possible to get at the opening, through which the sea poured in a cataract.

The removal of the wounded was therefore hurried, and every preparation made to leave the sinking vessel to her fate.

When the prisoners so far taken were marshaled on the Avenger's deck, it was found that, beside the wounded, seventeen of the Swiftwing's crew had been secured.

Captain Graham then ordered the cruiser to go after his other boats, which were still chasing two of the privateer's launches.

Bentham felt certain that Dick Powers was in one of the boats, and that both of them would be speedily overhauled was a foregone conclusion, as the moonlight was too bright to enable them to escape from the watchful eyes on board the cruiser.

Captain Graham paced the quarter-deck with a frown on his countenance.

He had absolutely nothing to show for his splendid victory but the consciousness of having rid his country of a dangerous craft, which but for this rencounter would soon having been preying upon American commerce, and with her splendid armament have carried things on with a high hand.

He had many prisoners, it was true, and others in the perspective, but they counted as nothing when compared with the value of the prize which was now rapidly going down.

Suddenly he bethought himself of the steamer which had showed English colors.

"Mr. Haskins," he said to the first lieutenant, "where's that sneaking steamer that was reported some time ago?"

"Off yonder, sir. Seems to be hanging round to pick up some of the privateer's crew. I noticed her edging down while we were engaged with the sinking steamer. I did not report it sooner, as I was of the opinion she was placing herself within our reach. She's in range of our long gun now, sir, and don't seem at all anxious to make off."

The captain examined the stranger carefully through his night-glass.

"It is strange," he said. "If that fellow isn't a blockade runner then I never saw one. He's got the cheek of the devil, but I'll make him explain himself in a few minutes. Mr. Haskins!"

"Yes, sir," said the officer, touching his cap.

"Pass the word for Mr. Bentham."

In two minutes the young gunner saluted his commander on he quarter-deck.

"You've been in Wilmington lately and are probably familiar with the looks of many of the blockade runners that were in that port at the time."

"I was only there one day, sir, and had little chance to inspect them ; but you may know that I came from Europe on one of the most notorious of the class."

"So I have heard. Well, sir, take this glass and examine yonder steamer and let me know what you think of her."

Bentham leveled the glass at the long, low, rakish vessel that was slowly sailing along in the bright moonlight, as though waiting for something, and hardly more than a mile distant.

"By George! that's the Foxhound, sir," he exclaimed excitedly.

"What!" ejaculated his commander, who knew the famous blockader well by reputation ; "the Foxhound ?"

"Yes, sir."

"Are you sure of that ?"

"Quite positive. She is the vessel I came over from France on, and is commanded by Captain Ralph Powell. She's loaded with cotton at this moment, or possibly she's just out of Nassau with contraband goods. In any case you will probably never have a better chance to bring her to."

"She's a prize worth the catching," said Captain Graham, briskly issuing orders to bear up for the stranger.

"Excuse me, sir, but it will interest you to know

that Powell has registered an oath never to be taken; for that exigency he carries a Whitehead torpedo in the hold of the Foxhound with a fuse attached leading to his stateroom. When capture seems unavoidable he will blow his vessel to the winds."

"He's a consummate donkey!" exclaimed Captain Graham. "He'll have an opportunity to do so now, I fancy. Do you know his speed?"

"Over sixteen knots when pressed, sir."

"Phew! We can't match that; but I guess we've a long reach in that pivot gun of yours, Mr. Bentham. Call your crew to quarters; everything will depend on your ability to cripple him as soon as he shows his heels."

"I will do my best, sir."

The young man touched his cap and retired to his station amidships.

"The boats have overhauled the privateer's launches, sir, and are towing them down," reported the first lieutenant at this juncture.

"We can't wait for them, Mr. Haskins. Signal them to follow in our wake. Ah, I see that fellow has waked up at last. He's heading for the Northwest Channel. That means he's bound for Nassau. Loaded to the decks with cotton, I guess. What a prize he'll make!"

And Captain Graham rubbed his hands gleefully.

The Avenger was run up to top speed, and for that matter so was the chase, for great clouds of black smoke issued from her funnel, and a long streak of foam was churned up by her screw.

"Let her have the pivot gun," exclaimed the commander.

Bertham sighted the gun carefully, the cruiser being held a point off the direct course, so as to offer no hindrance to the line of fire.

The lanyard was pulled, and a shell curved into the air, and finally exploded close to the Foxhound's stern.

"Good," cried the skipper. "Another like that, only a little closer, will disàble her screw."

" The captain of yonder craft has wonderful nerve, though I call it foolhardiness, to venture so close within range of an enemy," remarked Mr. Haskins.

"That's Powell's reputation ; he's a regular daredevil, they say. He had some object in hanging about here and taking such chances. He's a faster steamer than the Avenger, and will get away as it is, unless we can bring him to with a shot."

The next shell exploded high above the blockade runner's deck, but the third carried away the mizzentopmast.

The long gun was worked as rapidly as possible, but the Foxhound was not hit, and to Bentham's extreme vexation was gradually drawing away.

Great Abaco light was now visible above the horizon, and unless something was shortly done the blockade runner would reach the safety of the three-mile limit, and could not legally be overhauled.

During the next half hour three shells struck the fleeing steamer, but her speed was not affected in any way.

Twenty minutes later she was nearly out of range and fast nearing land, so the captain of the Avenger reluctantly hauled off and headed back over his course in order to pick up his boats.

On board of the Foxhound the engines were pounding like mad, and her furnaces were packed with tar and rosin.

"Ease her," exclaimed Captain Powell to his pilot, "yonder cruiser has given up the chase and gone about."

"Ay, ay, sir," and the bell in the engine-room rang out the joyful signal to slow up.

"A narrow shave, Powell; but a miss is as good as a mile any day."

The speaker was a fine-looking man, whose face was turned seaward.

"I should have been very sorry if this had turned out disastrously," he continued, "since I am responsible for putting you into the lion's den, so to speak. Had you not laid to to pick me up, after my vessel was knocked out, you would have been long since out of reach of the Yankee fangs; but I should have been a prisoner of war. I assure you that I am very grateful for your kindness. I could hardly expect another man to risk so much, even for a friend, and we, sir, are scarcely acquaintances."

"Say no more, Captain Powers; I am glad to have had an opportunity of doing you a service—not to speak of cheating the Yankees of an important prisoner of war."

"If I can ever return the favor, command me," said the late captain of the Swiftwing.

"What do you mean to do now?" said Powell.

"Get another ship and pay them back!" was the quick reply, as the speaker's eyes flashed and his hands clinched at the ends of his gray sleeves. "By my soul! Powell, I will make the Yankees suffer for this disaster."

"I hope you will, cap'n ; upon my soul I do."

"I forgot to tell you that the man you brought over from France, Bob Bentham, is chief gunner on yonder cruiser."

"How do you know that?" said Powell, not a little astonished.

"I have means of learning many things that it is to my interest to be informed of. Mr. Mowbray's instructions included positive orders to hunt out the craft that his nephew went to sea in, and unless she proved to be of much superior force I was to engage her at all hazards, and if possible put an end to that young man's career."

"You surprise me," said Powell.

"Well, when I left Wilmington, I found that the Swiftwing was unseaworthy. Mowbray had evidently been imposed upon when he purchased the vessel. I was forced to put into Nassau for safety. The privateer underwent a thorough examination in dry dock and was overhauled and put into A1 condition. I also obtained a heavier deck battery. In the meantime I was expecting intelligence regarding Bentham's movements. Yesterday I got a letter saying that this young man had been appointed to the Avenger—a fast steam cruiser of the third class, intended to over-haul the more important Confederate privateers. Like the Swiftwing she carried a broadside of four heavy guns, and a long rifled Parrott in the waist. There was not much difference in the armament of either vessel, so I felt easy in my mind about tackling her. My surprise, however, was great to run athwart her so soon. My only regret is that I lost the day."

"It was a most unfortunate Waterloo for you," said Powell.

"What galls me is that Bentham is aware that I commanded the Swiftwing. He bears me no good will, and the sinking of my vessel must have sent joy to his soul. But I will bide my time, and ere long I hope to return the compliment with interest."

"To which I respond amen, since the object of your animosity is a Yankee. Aside from that fact I must admit I admire that young Bentham for his courage and firmness in the hour of peril. But for him the Foxhound's ribs would now be ornamenting the shoals off Wilmington, and the Confederate government would have been poorer by a couple of million dollars worth of war material."

There was a pause in the conversation.

Since that terrible affair in the cabin, which I spoke to you about, the murder of Mr. Mowbray by Flash Gilmor, ill fortune has been our luck. We've been storm-struck for three days, but for which we had now been at Nassau unloading our cotton and figuring upon a fresh run."

"I wish I had Flash Gilmor here!" hissed Powers. "I'd hang him to your yard-arm, Powell, and if you interfered, by Jove! I'd take your life! You were going to convey him to Nassau?"

"Yes. At Nassau I would have turned him over to the authorities, and he would have been hustled back to Wilmington. But he got away."

"Unaided?" And Powers fixed his dark eyes on the captain of the Foxhound.

"I am afraid no," was the answer, in a lower tone. "Captain Powers, I haven't the same crew I once had. When I recruited after my last tussle with the block-aders, I was compelled to take some doubtful characters. I dared not investigate Flash Gilmor's escape on the high seas. When I get to Nassau I shall discharge my bad men and get better ones. I tell you that Gilmor had assistance. It was a cold-blooded crime."

"Not perpetrated in self-defense, then?"

"No! I believe he came on board disguised as a Confederate agent for a dark purpose. He knew that he could never make Norah his wife while Mowbray lived. The old man hated him as he hated the North."

Powers was silent for a moment.

"How does Norah seem?" he asked at length.

"I don't see her often; she keeps her stateroom," was Powell's answer. "During the fight this evening she sent the steward up to ask we what it all meant. That was the first I'd heard from her to-day."

"With your permission I'll go down and see her," said Captain Powers eagerly.

Powell made no reply.

"Do you object, Captain Powell?" inquired the Confederate officer, somewhat taken aback by his companion's silence.

"You promise not to excite her?"

"Certainly, sir. I might say I have a right to an interview since, with her late father's consent, I am a suitor for her hand."

"Oh, is it possible," said Powell. "The steward will show you her stateroom; but for all that she may not receive you."

"Oh, that is my risk, of course," said the handsome officer as he turned away and went down the companion-way.

Captain Powell paced his deck in silence, thinking probably of his good fortune in getting back to Nassau with a valuable load of cotton.

As he was a large owner in the Foxhound, it may be reasonably surmised that having made nine round trips he was very comfortably fixed—very rich in fact.

His home was at Nassau, where he lived in an unostentatious manner when on shore.

His niece, Miss Dora Maxwell, kept house for him, in a charming little cottage in the suburbs.

He knew she was eagerly awaiting the arrival of the Foxhound, for he had been away an unusually long time—his trip to Europe and return having occupied many weeks, and his delay at Wilmington several more—so that it was quite four months since he last saw the only relative he had in the world.

Perhaps Captain Powell was also thinking how he would excuse himself in the matter of Flash Gilmor's escape in an open boat on the night of his dastardly crime.

But he was not to blame for that.

The murderer had been manacled and secured below decks.

He could not have escaped without outside assistance, and this he had, as the captain had indicated to Captain Powers.

Indeed, Flash Gilmor had many accomplices on board, whom he was taking to Nassau in his pay, and for a purpose of his own not shown on the surface.

The identity of these fellows was suspected, but could not be proven, and therefore nothing could be done in the matter.

While the skipper of the Foxhound was pacing the

weather side of his quarter-deck, Captain Dick Powers sought the steward and was shown to the stateroom occupied by Miss Norah Mowbray.

He knocked for admission.

After a moment or two he heard a light footstep, which set his heart beating.

"Who is there?" said a sadly sweet voice.

"A friend," said Captain Powers.

"I don't recognize your voice, sir."

"I have only just come on board, Miss Mowbray. I am here with Captain Powell's permission."

There was a pause, and then the door was cautiously opened, showing the faultless figure of the late Gordon Mowbray's ward.

As her eyes fell on the face of her visitor she started.

"Merciful heavens!" she exclaimed, "it is Captain Powers!"

CHAPTER XVIII.

THE PRIVATEER'S OATH.

NORAH stood, pale-faced and full of emotion, in Captain Powers' presence.

Neither seemed disposed to break the silence that had followed the girl's last words.

Finally the Confederate officer said:

"I have heard the sad news, and I deeply regret the villain's escape. I shall follow him and avenge your father's death."

"No," said Norah gently, but with great firmness. "Leave him to the vengeance of Heaven. It will overtake him in its own good time. From whence did you come? Am I near the Swiftwing?"

"Alas! no," answered Powers, his brow darkening at thought of the privateer's destruction. "We met with the enemy, and the Swiftwing is at the bottom of the sea."

"It is well that *he* did not live to hear your report, for he expected great things of the ship—and of the commander," she added, with the faintest of smiles.

Powers did not answer for a moment.

"Never mind!" he suddenly cried. "In another vessel I will retrieve our fortunes, and the victory gained by our foes over the Swiftwing shall prove the dearest one of their lives. I am Captain Powell's passenger to Nassau. When I leave that port I will be on the quarter-deck of a new Destroyer—which shall literally sweep the seas."

He spoke these words in the voice of a man who loves to think of vengeance.

Rage leaped from the depths of his dark eyes, and he stood before the Southern beauty the very incarnation of grim resolution.

All the while the Foxhound was flying through the waters with the speed of a gale. Her engines sent her swiftly and noiselessly forward.

So well was she balanced on the waves, and so neatly built, that to Norah in her cozy little stateroom she was not moving at all.

Never before had the girl looked so lovely to Powers.

This was the woman whom he would make his wife —the beautiful creature whom Mowbray was to have given him when he had brushed Bob Bentham from his (Mowbray's) path.

Her guardian had been taken away, and she was thrown upon her own resources, left alone in the world with an immense fortune and an unpledged hand.

These things passed rapidly through the Confederate captain's mind.

" Your journey will end for the present at Nassau ?" said Powers, half-questioningly, fixing his eyes on his fair auditor.

" It will. I shall remain there an indefinite length of time—perhaps until the close of the war," was the response.

" It will last a long time."

" Perhaps."

" The South has not yet taxed her full strength."

"Neither has the national government."

Powers could not avoid noting the manner of her reply. It drew a stare from his eyes.

"I see that my words have surprised you," said Norah. "They seem to tell you that my sympathies are not with the government you serve."

"They indicate this, but I have not interpreted your words correctly. You have grown up under Gordon Mowbray's roof, and your hopes cannot be elsewhere. than with the South."

"Pardon me, sir, but if I have grown up as you say under the Mowbray roof, I have had thoughts—sentiments of my own. This is not the proper place for an open avowal of sentiments which you may call treason, but since we have advanced to where we stand, let me say that the movement of secession finds no sympathy with me. I am for the old flag; my heart, my hopes, and my wishes are with the Union."

A silence followed the girl's last words.

Captain Powers appeared thunderstruck.

"Then the loss of the Swiftwing occasions no regrets in your bosom," he said, coloring. "Recollect that its loss shortens your fortune by almost one hundred and fifty thousand dollars."

"The men who sunk with the vessel have my tears," she said softly; "but the loss of the money invested in her I do not regret. You will say that my avowed sentiments will deprive me of the estate which would naturally come into my possession by my father's death; that it will be confiscated by the Confederate government. He left no will, but many things have been understood for years. Captain Powers, I shall not lift a finger to retain those possessions. Let the Confederacy take them. My father's whole soul was wrapped up in the Southern cause ; he would have beggared himself for it. Men—his enemies—would have made out that he wavered, that his heart was not in the cause ; but a truer man to the South than he never lived. He will not see the humiliation of the government you serve, Captain Powers ; therefore it is well, perhaps, that the blue sea covers him."

"It is well, too, that he has not lived to see you arrayed on the side of the power he so cordially hated," said Powers bitterly. "You will not find any Northern sentiment prevailing at Nassau."

"I shall not court society of any kind while there," was the gentle answer. "You forget, Captain Powers, that the terrible deed committed on board this ship has darkened more than one page of my life history. I loved Gordon Mowbray, and to-night I throw the mantle of charity upon his faults."

Norah's eyes became suffused with tears as she finished.

Captain Powers watched her with the eyes of the eagle that sees a dove in his power.

He threw a rapid glance over his shoulder and stepped forward.

"Ah ! if you would but bestow upon others a tithe of the love he drew from you !" he said, in tones that lifted the girl's gaze to his face.

" What do you mean "'

" Have you been blind till this time ?" was the quick, passionate response. " Norah, I stand before you a self-confessed lover. I have loved you with all the depth and the ardor of my soul, and I here, for the first time, trust my lips with the declaration. I have Mowbray's promise, but I would win you myself."

Norah's look checked him.

"Was not that promise a bargain as well?" she asked.

Captain Powers started.

"Come," she continued, smiling. "Confess, Captain Powers, that you were to have me for certain work on the high seas. Ah! I know a good deal about the purpose of the Swiftwing. There were secrets in Mowbray House, but some were not well kept. It was a bargain as well as a promise."

The captain stood perplexed in the fair creature's presence, but his audacity came to the rescue.

"Promise or bargain, it may yet be kept," he exclaimed.

"Sir?"

"I would not be misunderstood now, not for the world!" he continued quickly. "You have not answered my declaration of love——"

"Need I answer?"

"It is not necessary;" and his lips closed behind the last word. "It was the desire of the dead that you should become my wife, Norah, and my life mission shall be to fulfill it. My love for you is not abated by our meeting to-night; it has become intensified. I like a hard conquest, a well-fought battle, where there is much at stake. I shall make you my wife! I shall triumph in this tilt for a heart at the altar!"

Norah's eyes flashed defiance before she replied. They accepted his challenge.

"Captain Powers, I am not surprised at your words," she said, assuming a calmness which she evidently did not possess. "They are the natural outgrowth of de-sires nursed in secret, but boldly proclaimed to a young girl whom murder has left unprotected. So you will make me your wife? We will stand at an altar deco-rated with the Confederate flags, while pæons of vic-tory float skyward over the ruins of the Federal Union! This is one of your dreams, I suppose. Let me break it; for I say here that hour of your triumph will never come! I will never, never, become your wife. The promise and the bargain must fall fruitless to the ground."

Captain Powers could not but admire the fair girl who spoke these words.

She stood before him as lovely as a queen, with courage beaming from the depths of her deep, sorrow-ful eyes, and with her figure drawn to its full stature.

The captain of the ill-fated privateer could not see the stooped figure of the man who listened on the out-side of the stateroom door.

" By Jove! I carry a Yankee lover!" ejaculated the eavesdropper, who had a figure like Captain Powell's. "I never dreamed that old Mowbray's ward would ever think of such a thing. What will Dick Powers say now? I think the girl has put an end to the argument."

The man was the captain of the Foxhound.

A minute's silence followed Norah's last sentence.

" Oh, we will see who wins!" suddenly exclaimed Powers. "Do not think that I expect to lose the game. Gordon Mowbray was my friend. I respect the promise of the dead, and I swear to-night on the deep, blue waters of this tropical sea that Gordon Mowbray's last oath shall be kept."

A defiant laugh was the girl's only reply.

"You fling down the gauntlet, my beauty; "but it only goads me forward to victory!" he said. "I know where your heart is, but I will cross swords with Bob Bentham on his own deck ere long and show him that the arm he struck down on the bauks of the Cape Fear River can deal blows of vengeance. Love and live for him, if you will. Here in Nassau you will find few whose hearts beat for our enemies. To this place Bentham dare not come. Ah, the coward! he will keep behind iron plates and surround himself with ten-inch guns! I long to meet him! I will find him if I have to seek him in the midst of a Yankee fleet."

"He will not shun the meeting—be sure of that, Captain Powers," said the girl calmly. "Look out— he might turn hunter himself. Stranger things than this have happened."

Captain Powers vouchsafed no reply, but turned suddenly toward the door.

"Good-night," he said, as he reached the threshold. "I will keep my oath! You shall become the wife of Captain Powers yet."

He flung wide the door as he concluded, and so suddenly that the eavesdropper on the outside failed to escape discovery.

"What! a listener?" exclaimed Powers, springing madly after the Foxhound's captain, whom he quickly overtook, and whirled until they stood face to face. "By my soul! it is Powell!"

"It is Powell!" echoed the blockade runner. "I owe you no apology, captain. I gave you orders when you left me not to excite that young girl, and I followed you to see that my orders were obeyed."

"Well?"

The one word was accompanied by an eye challenge.

"You touched forbidden ground, but the girl stood it bravely. She's more than a match for you, captain. You'll never win her!"

"By heavens! I will!" was the quick retort. "I have never failed in a love affair, and I've had more than one. If you say so, Powell, I'll go back, and repeat my oath, sealing it with a kiss."

"Not while she is my passenger?" exclaimed Powell. "You have said enough to her to-night—more than I think a gentleman would have said. This is my ship, captain, and Norah is my passenger. She's Yankee in sentiment, but she has a right to think as she pleases. I say you shan't disturb her any more. Her stateroom is to be invaded no more twixt here and port."

Captain Powers stared into the speaker's face revealed by the ship's lantern that swung overhead.

Powell was desperately in earnest.

"Ho—ho, Powell!" he laughed, almost boisterously, "I've a motion to go back just to try you."

"You'd better not!" and Captain Powell's hand touched Powers' arm. "There are some things you can't do on board this ship. I am master here. When you rouse me, you stir up a tiger!"

That was the end of it.

Powers did not go back.

CHAPTER XIX.

DORA AND NORAH.

THE Foxhound continued her course until Nassau was reached.

Threatened by Captain Powell's look and voice, Dick Powers had not sought a second interview with Norah, and the girl kept within her stateroom.

Day was breaking again when the little blockade runner entered the port with the Confederate flag flying. She soon came to anchor, and Powell went below to tell Norah that the city had been reached.

The distressed girl received him with a smile, glad to know that she was to leave the ship; even though she was about to take up her residence in a city where but few hearts beat for the American Union.

As Captain Powell assisted her politely upon deck her eyes sent an inquiring glance round the ship, as though she sought some one.

" You will be spared the sight of Captain Powers," said the blockade runner, addressing her. " He bade me a hasty good-by twenty minutes ago, and has already disappeared. It was well for him that he went no further than he did last night."

" You were near, then ?"

Powell's face flushed.

" I was at the door," he said. " I believe it is the first time I ever played eavesdropper on board my own ship, but I had told Captain Powers that you were not to be excited. I was afraid he might go too far. You will pardon me for listening, Miss —— ?"

"Certainly," smiled Norah. "Captain Powell, you have heard me declare my sentiments. They are not in accordance with yours."

"You've a full right to them," answered the Confederate quickly. "I'm a full-blooded Confederate, Miss Norah. I would sink every Yankee ship afloat if I had the power, but I never begrudge a woman her sentiments—never! Of course I did not expect to hear you talk as you have, since you were raised under Mowbray's roof; but if you like the old flag better than the new one, why, stick to it."

Norah was about to reply, thanking Captain Powell for his words; but they had reached the ship's side, and were about to descend to the boat waiting for them on the calm waters of the bay.

"Have you any acquaintances in Nassau ?" he asked of Norah, as the boat put off.

"None at all. I come to the city a stranger "

Powell seemed to reflect a moment.

"Would you let me recommend a friend?" he said.

"Indeed I would, and thank you besides."

"I have a niece here—a young lady about your age," he continued. "I am sure you two would get along famously together. Dora was raised in the tropics, and I call her a real tropic flower. She will talk what you might call treason, Norah ; but for all that you'll like her."

Norah was much delighted to know that she would not be isolated in a strange land.

She believed she would like Captain Powell's niece, and longed to meet her.

She thus expressed herself to the blockade runner, who seemed delighted, and a few minutes later Norah was in Nassau.

The arrival of the Foxhound had attracted quite a crowd of people to the quay, and the sight of a young and handsome woman in the captain's boat caused a murmur of speculation to float from lip to lip.

The fair young girl stood the stares of the crowd for some time without complaining.

At length she turned to Captain Powell with a smile:

"Do they always stare thus at your passengers, captain?" she asked.

"Bless you! no, girl. A lady passenger on board the Foxhound is, indeed, a novelty. They all know Dora, and they are wondering whether or not you are to supplant her in my heart."

Norah met Captain Powell's glance with a blush, seeing which the blockade runner broke into a laugh.

"No harm intended at any rate, Norah," he said. "Dora is the only woman who can have Powell's love. We will see her soon."

The people cheered Powell as he passed along; for he was known as the most daring as well as the most successful blockade runner sailing from Nassau.

Many a rich cargo had he conveyed to the Confederates.

His daring ventures had brought much gold to Nassau, and, if the war lasted many months, he would enrich many of her citizens.

"They rather like the old blockade runner here," he smiled to Norah, as he lifted his cap in response to the plaudits of the crowd.

The young girl did not reply.

At that moment she had caught sight of a pair of dark eyes fastened upon her like the orbs of a basilisk.

They were just raised above the shoulder of a man, so that she could not see the lower part of the face.

A strange and nameless thrill shot to Norah's heart while the eyes regarded her, and she was returning their glare with a questioning look when Captain Powell spoke the words last recorded.

Did the blockade runner notice the eyes?

He glanced at Norah, wondering why she had not replied, and his look wandered back to the crowd through which they were still passing.

Presently the evil black eyes vanished, perhaps because Norah had passed on, but she could not forget them.

They had welcomed her to Nassau in a manner not at all desirable. Had she ever seen them before?

The fair girl thought of Flash Gilmor and shivered.

Not long afterward Captain Powell rapped on the door of a small frame house which had a beautiful little flower garden in front, and a moment later a vision of loveliness appeared on the threshold.

A sylph's figure and a houri's face—that is what appeared to Norah.

We would describe the person as a tall young girl of eighteen, with a soft olive complexion, black hair, and large lustrous eyes, such as one often meets with in the tropics.

She greeted the blockade runner with an exclamation of joy which soon became an enthusiastic welcome; but in the midst of her demonstrations she suddenly caught sight of Norah and started.

"I have brought you a companion, Dora," said Powell, glancing at Norah.

"A companion and a friend; how glad I am!" exclaimed Dora, turning from Powell and grasping Norah's hands, while she drew near for a kiss. "We will be friends forever! I have been lonely a long time, and you could have brought me no grander present than this friend, Uncle Ralph."

Powell smiled proudly as the two girls embraced, and Dora, clinging to Nora's hand, led the way into the house.

The interior of the building was in keeping with the outside; exotic plants and flowers everywhere, and on every hand a certain beauty and neatness which proclaimed loving woman's rule.

Norah was soon left alone with her new acquaintance, for Powell left to go back to the ship, where he knew he would be wanted to pay off the men whom he expected to discharge.

The two girls sat in the cosy room that looked out upon the street, Dora still touching Norah's hand tenderly and gazing with sisterly affection into her face.

"Now, tell me all," she said, in a tone which drew from Mowbray's ward a full recital of her life since leaving Wilmington.

Dora listened without once interrupting her fair narrator. She breathlessly followed her, word by word, and sat silent for a moment after the story.

"I know this Flash Gilmor," were Dora's first words, spoken in a tone that startled Norah. "I have seen the ruffian!" and the girl's small hands clinched. Let us hope that the waters ingulfed him and the boat he stole; that the ocean avenged your father's death. Once I was seated at this very window, looking out upon the street, half dreaming, half dozing. It was a lovely day, like the many we have in Nassau. All at once a pair of eyes became fixed upon me. I saw them peering through the plants in the window like the eyes of a snake. I could not think that they belonged to a man, yet I knew that they were not a serpent's orbs. I leaned forward, intending to bid the intruder begone, when a young man doffed his hat and bowed. That was my introduction to Flash Gilmor. I afterward discovered that he had come to Nassau in a blockade runner for the purpose of winning a bet which he had made at Charleston—that he would marry Captain Powell's niece within three months."

Nora could hardly repress an exclamation of surprise.

"You may be sure that he lost his money," continued Dora, with a laugh. "He would have entered this house then if I had not given Pedro, my Spanish servant, orders to let no serpents cross the threshold. I spoke the command in a tone intended solely for Flash Gilmor's ears, and he shrunk away abashed. He came back, however, and let slip no opportunity of throwing himself in my path; but I made him the laughing stock of Nassau until a Confederate vessel carried him away. Since then I have not seen him, and your mention of him, Norah, has been the first time I have heard his name spoken for many a week."

The two girls continued to converse until a servant called Dora from the parlor, leaving Norah alone.

Mowbray's ward arose and went to the window for

the purpose of inspecting a rare flower, which had commanded her praise for several minutes.

She soon found herself admiring the profusion of exotics that bloomed around her, filling the whole room with their fragrance, and forming a bower of great beauty.

An exclamation escaped Norah's lips as she caught sight of a flower, the most beautiful of all she had yet seen; but it hung out of the window, yet within reach.

Norah leaned forward to lift the flower gently, in order that she might become fully acquainted with its exquisite loveliness.

All at once a hand encircled her waist, and the form of a man rose before her.

A glance showed the girl his handsome face and evil black eyes.

A wild cry pealed from her throat, and the next moment she had fallen to the floor in a swoon, in which state Dora found her a few moments later.

CHAPTER XIX.

CAPTAIN POWELL KEEPS HIS OATH.

AFTER the fruitless chase of the Foxhound, Captain Graham picked up his boats, and laid his course for Charleston to report to the admiral of the station the result of his first marine duel, and to deliver his prisoners that they might be sent North.

He was in particular good humor, for the first clause in his sealed instructions, directing him to hang about the Bahamas and capture or destroy the steamer Swiftwing, before she could get away upon her lawless errand, had been fulfilled to the letter.

The Avenger had been roughly handled in the late fight, but not so badly but the carpenters and machinists on board could soon repair all damages.

But some things were beyond repair—a dozen hardy Yankee tars lay on the lower deck in a row sewed up in their hammocks ready for the solemn service that was presently to consign them to the universal watery churchyard where no tombstones mark the last resting places of many thousands of the wanderers on the trackless deep.

It was on the evening of the day following that the Avenger approached the Yankee squadron off Charleston.

It was pretty dark on the water, as the sky was overcast by clouds, and a half-gale was blowing, kicking up a tolerably nasty sea.

The first intimation that Captain Graham had of the immediate presence of the blockading fleet was a rocket sent up by a vigilant gunboat.

It was green and red, signifying in the signal code that a suspicious steamer was in sight. Of course this meant the Avenger.

Shortly afterward a blue light was to be seen directly ahead from another craft, and as soon as it burned out three lanterns appeared in the rigging in the form of a triangle—a red one at the top and a white and a green one at the bottom.

Captain Graham had no need to call for his code to interpret this signal—as plain as a pikestaff it read to his eye " who are you?"

The signal ensign was immediately instructed to answer it.

Soon after the Avenger ran close to the "Firefly" gunboat.

In answer to Captain Graham's inquiry for the admiral of the station, he was directed to a point inshore where the flagship—a large sailing frigate—was snugly anchored.

The Avenger proceeded slowly landward and presently made out the big cruiser, with her frowning tier of guns run out in readiness for any emergency.

"Steamer ahoy!" came a sharp hail from the flagship, showing that the lookouts were wide awake.

"Ahoy!" replied Captain Graham.

"What steamer is that?"

"Screw steamer Avenger, Captain Graham, from the Bahama station. Tell the admiral that I am coming on board."

"Very well, sir."

Lights flashed on the deck of the flagship and preparations made to receive the visitor according to his rank.

The first cutter of the Avenger was piped away, and the commander of the cruiser was soon in the admiral's cabin.

Captain Graham found that august personage making himself comfortable over a whiskey punch.

The report made by the cruiser's captain was eminently satisfactory to the admiral, who congratulated him upon his success.

As the Avenger was a remarkably fast vessel the admiral said he would take the liberty of supplementing the instructions of the Navy Department, by ordering Graham to delay his cruise after the Shenandoah privateer, and give attention to the Foxhound blockade runner.

The admiral said that he had been censured in common with his brother admiral on the Wilmington station for their want of success in putting an end to this particular vessel, which continued to run the blockade off both ports with the greatest impunity.

He said Graham must watch for the steamer, and run him down or sink him, and the commander of the cruiser, promising to do his best in the matter, took his leave.

About noon on the following day the Avenger got away and headed straight for the Northeast passage in the Bahamas, where Captain Graham proposed to lie off and on until the Foxhound made her appearance from Nassau with a fresh load of contraband goods on board.

It was night again on the broad expanse of the tropical sea, about three weeks after the incidents already narrated.

The cruiser Avenger was steaming slowly along well inside of Great Abaco light.

It was not very dark, though the moon was still below the horizon, for the stars were out in all their glory.

"She won't come out to-night, that's certain," said Bentham to Jupe, with whom he was conversing, while both hung over the starboard bulwarks in the waist of the steamer.

"By golly, Marse Bob, I dunno 'bout dat. Dat yere Powell is de mos' recklus pusson I eber know'd. Ebery udder skipper hangs back for a foggy ebening, but dat Powell, he don't seem ter care a snap. De Foxhound is so debblish fast dat he snap him fingers at de cruisers here 'bouts, and come an' go when him please. I reckon dat him bery suah ter come out if him make up him mind ter do so."

"Well, if he does, we'll nab him as sure as eggs are eggs."

"Golly, I hope so, sah."

"Steamer ho !" came pealing down from the foretop, startling every one into alertness.

The officer of the deck soon learned that the stranger was several miles distant, and was stealing seaward, close under the lee of Eleuthera island.

Not a light showed aboard of her, and she looked like a thin black moving shadow ; indeed, it required very sharp eyes indeed to make her out at all until attention was called to the spot.

Several night-glasses were leveled at her.

"I'll bet that's the Foxhound. Powell is a sly

rascal, and calculates that we won't expect him on such a bright night," said Captain Graham to Mr. Haskins, his lieutenant. "Well, we'll have to cut him off or he'll get away again."

The cruiser's nose was laid for a certain point ahead of the stranger, and Bentham ordered to call his gun's crew to quarters.

The furnace doors in the hold were thrown wide open, and the slumbering flames fed with the contents of several tar barrels, and then the stokers proceeded to shovel in coal at a lively rate.

The Avenger swooped down upon her prey like a falcon, and thoughts of prize money began to loom before the mental vision of all on board.

"I'll bet dat's him for suah, Massa Bob," exclaimed Jupe, as he laid down the sponger with which he had been cleaning the bore of the huge Parrott rifle.

"I hope so," returned Bentham earnestly.

"Golly, we is gwine ter cut him off dis yere time, an' doan' yer forget it," said the darky, forgetting himself in his joy and cutting a "pigeon wing" upon the deck.

Before long it was seen that the stranger, whoever he was, had wore round and turned back toward Nassau, as though her commander had concluded now that his presence was discovered that it was too risky to run out to sea, and was acting upon the maxim that discretion was the better part of valor.

The position of the Avenger, however, was such that she could cut the distant steamer off in either direction, or at least come within easy gun range.

It was eleven o'clock when Bentham was instructed to throw a shot at her.

"Old Abe" was carefully sighted by the young gunner, and then Jupe pulled the lanyard with great unction.

The shell soared aloft and burst close to the fleeing steamer.

Shot followed shot after that, and finally one shell struck the blockade runner squarely in the stern.

After that she seemed to be crippled, for the cruiser came down on her hand over hand.

"Hit, by the Lord Harry!" exclaimed Captain Graham.. "She's ours. By my soul, the men will get their first prize-money to-night."

"Old Abe" had done his duty, and there was no need to discharge another shell.

The stranger was drifting ashore.

The two steamers were now less than a mile apart.

A full-orbed moon hung over the wide expanse of waters, silvering the crests of the waves, and affording the Union vessel plenty of light.

With full head on, the Avenger now bore swiftly down upon the blockade runner, still endeavoring to escape, despite the injuries inflicted by Bentham's gun.

Everybody on board the Union cruiser was on the alert.

Ten minutes later the Avenger ran alongside, and the voice of Captain Graham was plainly heard as he called out:

"Ship ahoy! Who are you?"

The reply was not delayed an instant.

"The steamer Foxhound,"

"Great heaven!" ejaculated Bentham to Jupe. "Powell may keep his oath?"

"We are the United States cruiser, Avenger,"

answered the young commander. "Do you sur-render?"

A moment of breathless suspense followed.

"We are not armed. Your shot has pierced us through and through," was the response. "We cannot resist and are forced to surrender."

The next moment a loud voice on the Confederate's deck cried out:

"Into the sea for your lives, men! The captain has fired the fuse attached to the torpedo!"

Instantly dark figures leaped over the sides of the blockade runner and threw themselves into the sea.

"I feared that!" exclaimed Bentham, making for the quarter-deck. "For heaven's sake back off, Captain Graham. There's no telling when the torpedo will explode!"

The Avenger was instantly reversed, and the next moment she was leaving the spot as rapidly as possible.

All at once a noise like the explosion of a score of ammunition chests rent the air, the very sea itself seemed to reel, and the Avenger was almost thrown upon her side.

Captain Ralph Powell of the Foxhound had kept his word!

His famous ship was worse than a wreck.

With his own hands he had destroyed her rather than let her fall into the hands of the Unionists.

If the Avenger had not been warned by the voice from the Foxhound's deck she might have been sunk by the explosion, for Powell had evidently waited until she came up for the mad purpose of sinking both ships together.

The force of the explosion prostrated every soul on board the Union cruiser.

Strong men fell in all directions.

Bentham was thrown across a gun-carriage, and Graham was knocked senseless by a spar that swept the quarter-deck.

For several minutes not a man spoke.

There were cries for help from the sea.

Boats were lowered as quickly as possible, and a number of the crew of the Foxhound were pulled from the sea, more frightened than hurt.

"The old ship's gone at last," said one of the rescued men when he found his breath among his rescuers. "To think that we've been sailing the seas eight months with a torpedo somewhere in the hold ready to blow us to perdition! Some thought the captain wouldn't keep his word, but I knew him better than all the rest of them. When he went below half an hour ago with his two hands clinched and his eyes flashing, I knew that the Foxhound would never carry another cargo."

"Where's Captain Powell?" asked Bentham at the first opportunity.

"I guess you'll have to ask the sea," was the reply. "He's just lucky enough to escape on a spar, you see land is close aboard, and live to run the blockade till the war closes."

"After blowing up one ship?" ejaculated the young gunner.

"That's my opinion, sir. I've got confidence enough in Captain Powell's luck to believe in things you'd never dream of."

CHAPTER XX.

A DANGEROUS MISSION.

THE sea for some distance around the spot where the Foxhound had met her fate at the hands of her mad captain was strewn with fragments of the disaster.

The captured sailor's words impressed Bentham.

He did not, therefore, scour the sea in a boat in a vain search for Powell, but contented him with picking up a sailor now and then, and at last rowed back to the Avenger.

The men of the Foxhound told Graham that they had lately cleared at Nassau with a cargo consisting of army clothing, besides a lot of medical stores for the Confederate army, that they did not expect to run across the Avenger, which they understood had departed on a cruise in search of the privateer Shenandoah. They said that Bentham's last shot had disabled their engines, besides killing three men.

Thanks to that shot, the sea had been rid of a pest, and the swiftest blockade runner in the Confederate service was at the bottom of the deep.

Bentham then learned for the first time that the Foxhound had picked Captain Powers up after the sinking of the Swiftwing, and taken him to Nassau, where he was getting ready to go to sea as the commander of a strong vessel named the Destroyer, which English gold had purchased and manned.

"Good!" exclaimed the young gunner, when he learned this. "I shall yet meet Powers on the deck of a Confederate privateer—just where I have longed to encounter him."

The talkative prisoners also informed Cannoneer Bob of Norah's trip to Nassau; and, little by little, the story of the terrible tragedy in the Foxhound's cabin was told.

We need not say that the gunner hung on each word with breathless interest.

What! Mowbray dead—murdered—and Norah in Nassau, a stranger in a strange city?

What trials, what indignities would not assail her there!

"The prisoners do not attempt to shield Flash Gilmor," he said to himself, when he found himself alone. "They cannot. He killed Uncle Gordon in cold blood, and for a purpose as base as his own dark heart. I wish Jupe had finished him that night on the river bank. It would have prevented a murder, anyhow. But I still live! Beware, Flash Gilmor! You may yet encounter one whose sword will avenge the death of that impulsive old man! I will not believe that the sea ingulfed the murderer the night of his escape. Water does not drown men of his stripe. They live to feel the merciless stroke of a Nemesis."

In the quiet of his little quarters Bob Bentham stood alone thus communing with himself.

"I will go to Nassau," he said, with the air of a man who had formed a great resolution which is certain to bring him face to face with danger. "I feel that Norah will be surrounded by danger. Dick Powers is there. Flash Gilmor may soon confront

her with the glitter of victory in his eyes. Between
the two men she will suffer indignities which will call
for vengeance!"

Having said this he went to Graham's cabin and
started the young commander with the announcement
of his wish for a trip to Nassau.

"You go to Nassau?" exclaimed Captain Graham.
"Why, it is a veritable den of lions."

"I know that," answered the young gunner, smiling. "If it were a pen of lambs I might not decide to
go. My mind is made up, captain. I go to Nassau —
with your permisson."

Of course it was contrary to the regulations of the
service for Bentham to leave the ship except by ex-
press permission of his commander; but our hero had
reasons for believing that Captain Graham, when he
had heard his reasons, would not refuse him leave of
absence.

His commander heard him with patience and then
said:

"I don't know how I can spare you, Bentham, just
at this time. Your services are invaluable to me, for
my duty in these seas is accomplished, and the
Shenandoah, and other steamers of her class, now
demand my attention."

"I regret the necessity, sir; but to me the matter
is imperative. Of course it remains for you to say
whether you will permit me to go or not."

Captain Graham thought a moment.

"Well," he said, "it is a dangerous adventure, and
I strongly advise you against undertaking it; but I
know when a pretty woman has wound herself about
a young man's heart he will go through fire and

water for her sake. You may go, Bentham. I will put you ashore before morning. You will report to the admiral as soon as you can."

The Avenger fell in at daybreak the next day with a vessel bound for New York, and the men saved after the explosion of the blockade runner were transferred to her decks, and the two vessels parted company.

Graham regretted that he was not able to turn Ralph Powell over as a prisoner, for a possibility of his escape still remained.

Once in the hands of the government, he would never resume his daring operations on the high seas.

Having got rid of her prisoners, the Avenger headed for Nassau with the intention of approaching near enough to allow Bentham a chance to enter it.

Graham had hoped that sober second thought would break the gunner's resolution ; but it seemed only to strengthen it.

Norah, unprotected, was in Nassau. Dick Powers, the privateer, was there too.

Was not this enough to demand his presence there?

Bentham had also obtained permission for Jupe to go with him.

The two had seemingly united their fortunes, for Jupe was with Bentham when he served the guns of the Cumberland in her hopeless battle with the Merrimac, and ever since he had kept close to the loyal gunner's side.

It was early in the morning when the Avenger came to a short distance from Nassau, whose lights could be seen without the aid of a glass.

A boat was noiselessly lowered over the ship's side,

and the figure of a herculean negro sprung nimbly down the ladder.

"Be ever on the watch, Bentham," said Graham to the person who held out his hand previous to following the darky.

"You may know that I will not sleep in that treason-infected city," was the answer. "I shall not move without counting the cost. I have weighed everything carefully, captain. I enter Nassau with my eyes open."

"Good! I'm glad of that," was the reply, and the speaker's hand closed fervently on the one it grasped.

A few more words were spoken, and the young man who bade Captain Graham good-by descended to the boat, and gave a command in a whisper for it to put off.

Bentham's most intimate friends would hardly have recognized him as he sat in the bow of the ship's boat that night with his face turned toward the lights of Nassau.

He had doffed the uniform he had worn for weeks with credit and heroism, and now wore a simpler dress which would not be likely to attract attention in Nassau, nor rouse the suspicion of any one.

The boat propelled by muffled oars crept noiselessly through the water and swiftly approached the city.

Not a word was uttered by any one.

It glided across an unfrequented part of the harbor, easily avoiding the shipping, and at last touched the wharf at a deserted-looking place, for neither bale, box nor human being was to be seen.

After carefully inspecting the quay at the point

touched as well as they were able, Bentham and Jupe landed and the boat which had conveyed them to the city quietly put back toward the ship.

"Hyer we is, Massa Bob, in de hyena's den," said Jupe in the lowest of whispers. "If Cap'n Powers be in Nassa', why, Tom de black rascal must be hyar, too, an' de consequence am dat ole Jupe must be on the lookout."

"You certainly must, Jupe," observed Bentham, who instantly recalled the negro by whom his escape from Wilmington had nearly been frustrated, and then he added to himself. "I do not intend to submit myself to that sable villain's eyes for inspection if I can help it. I would sooner pass in review before Captain Powers himself."

Immediately after the boat's return to the Avenger, whose young captain was anxious to hear of his gunner's safe arrival in Nassau, Bentham and his faithful friend turned from the wharf.

It was not Bentham's first visit to Nassau.

He had spent several months in the city during his boyhood and when his father commanded a United States ship, but since that time the place had undergone numerous changes, although it had retained its general features.

He therefore had no difficulty in finding his way to the main portion of the town.

Jupe was at his heels.

"Massa Bob, we'se follered," suddenly said the darky in a startling whisper as his hand fell on Bentham's arm sending a thrill to his heart.

The loyal gunner instantly stopped.

It was a critical moment—a spy at his heels.

"Dar! de spy has stopped, too!" ejaculated Jupe. "It's a mighty good t'ing dat de street ain't lighted up, Massa Bob. Jes' you walk on a piece; den you'll heah de debbil come on agin."

Bentham moved forward with ears strained to catch the slightest sound, but he heard nothing.

"De spy hab taken off his shoes!" said Jupe.

CHAPTER XXI.

FEARLESS AND BRAVE.

THE young gunner instinctively reached for his revolver.

"It mustn't come to dat, Massa Bob," said the darky, clutching his wrist. "A pistol shot would spile de hull bizness. Dat spy must be got outen de way an' dat without much ceremony. Trust ole Jupe fo' dat. Jes' go on now, massa, wid walk enuff fo' two men. I'll fix de spy."

Seeing no other way out of the difficulty and repos-ing a world of confidence in Jupe, Bentham moved on again.

The darky crouched at the foot of a tree with his face turned toward the sea.

Without a single weapon in his hand, the giant negro waited for the person who was certainly on his master's trail.

Like a Numidian lion waiting for a straggler from a caravan the big black prepared to sieze his prey.

Deceived by Bentham's movements, the night spy came on again like a tiger sure of his victim.

Jupe did not move a muscle.

Presently his eyes singled out a gliding figure darker than the night itself, and advancing with the silken tread of the cat.

All at once the crouching negro rose and threw himself forward.

He landed against the unsuspecting spy whose throat one of his sable hands clutched, and whom he bore backward notwithstanding his desperate struggles.

"Not a word, you spyin' debbil!" hissed Jupe, in the trailer's ear. "De hand ob a giant am at your throat, an' you may find yerself in de world ob spirits mighty soon ef your tongue wags."

The spy could not speak, even if he had wished to, for his captor's hand almost choked him, and effectually prevented a single word from finding its way from his tongue.

At length Jupe thought he had choked the spy enough. He loosened his grip, but not until he had dragged him from the sidewalk into a narrow way not unlike an alley.

"Now, what you follerin' us fo'?" demanded Jupe.

A long breath, a gasp, and then:

"You'se Jupe, ole Massa Mowbray's nigger."

Jupe could hardly repress an exclamation of surprise.

The spy was Black Tom, the negro who had accompanied Captain Powers from Wilmington in the Swiftwing.

The surprise was mutual.

"I'se ole Jupe, suah enuff!" said Bentham's black companion, when he recovered from his surprise. Now, look hyer, Tom, who'se you spyin' fo' in Nassau?"

"Dat's my bizness!" was the provoking answer.

For a moment Jupe's hand seemed about to fly at the captive's throat again.

"No foolin', Tom," he said threateningly. "Dis am de most serious piece ob bizness you'se eber had to do with. I can't afford to let you go, fo' de man what you'se with now, Cap'n Powers, would know eberything afo' mornin'.'"

Tom said nothing.

The look that he gave Jupe was the glare of a tiger.

Not far off Bentham waited for the man he had left behind.

The two negroes had never been friends.

Hating each other as boys, they had grown to manhood as Mowbray's slaves with that hate intensified by petty rivalries and disputes, and now they stood face to face in a strange city, captor and captive, thirsting for each other's blood.

Jupe was not his enemy's superior in strength, but he had surprised him, and thus held an advantage gained by cunning.

"You habn't answered me, Tom," said Jupe, nettled by his enemy's silence. "You mustn't tell Cap'n Powers what you'se seen to-night."

"Yes, but I will, Jupe!"

With the last word the black captive broke suddenly away, and dealt his captor a blow that staggered him.

Prodigious as that blow was, it failed to place Jupe *hors de combat.* He almost instantly recovered, and bounded after his antagonist, who had sprung away.

Black Tom saw he was at his heels, and attempted to make his escape."

"You'se got to be my pris'ner yet!" grated Jupe, as the thought of Tom escaping with the information he had obtained rushed across his mind. "De angel ob vengeance am on yer track, Black Tom, an' you can't git away!"

Bentham heard the two men approach him.

The next moment they flitted past like specters, leaving him holding his breath, and with a revolver still half drawn.

Jupe was the better runner of the two blacks.

He gained on the sable spy so swiftly that Tom saw that escape could not be effected by running.

All at once he whirled with a hoarse, tigerish ejaculation, and confronted Jupe with uplifted knife.

"I'se knife proof, you spyin' nigger!" shot from Jupe's throat, as he sprung straight at his enemy, knocking the knife arm up and dealing him a blow that sent him reeling back.

Black Tom rose almost instantly, but Jupe grappled him, and the two sable giants writhed and twisted for a few moments in one of the most desperate struggles that can be imagined.

Bentham heard it on the darkened street, and bounded forward, eager to help terminate it in Jupe's favor, for discovery, if not arrest, was liable to take place at any moment.

When he reached the combatants one sprung up and confronted him.

" De spyin' debbil will nebber tell Cap'n Powers what him saw to-night," said the negro, pointing to the form lying motionless at his feet.

" You've killed him, Jupe."

" 'Spect so, Massa Bob. It am de only sure way ob stoppin' a spy's tongue. Remember dat we am in Nassau, an' dat Black Tom b'longs to Cap'n Dick Powers."

Bentham stooped over the spy for a moment and satisfied himself that he was dead.

He regretted that his entrance into Nassau had been

followed by the death of a human being, but by the taking of a life of but little moment to the world at large his own had been saved.

"We must go on, Jupe," he said to the giant negro, to whom he now owed lasting friendship. "There may be more spies in Nassau."

"Dat's a fact, Massa Bob. We must go on fo' suah."

Near where the two negroes had decided their combat was the mouth of a dark alley into which Jupe hastily dragged his foe.

When he rejoined Bentham there was an unmistakable gleam of victory in his eyes.

Bentham and his dusky companion now secured quiet lodgings, and as they were worn out for want of sleep they slept nearly all day, and night was falling fast when they once more came out upon the streets.

The twain hurried on without speaking, nor paused again until they reached one of the many squares of the city.

They found it well lighted and thronged with people, all of whom seemed in a merry mood, for news had been received of an important Confederate victory.

A great many Americans appeared everywhere among the crowds, and Bentham was constantly on the lookout.

"Look a leetle ober yer right shoulder, Massa Bob," suddenly said Jupe, in low tones, that did not reach any other ears than those for which they were spoken. "Take a squint at dat dar man standin' by de little officer."

Bentham looked in the direction indicated and saw two men—one below the average height, clad in Confederate naval uniform, the other tall, and dressed in a manner that suggested a disguise.

"Flash Gilmor!" fell from the gunner's lips, after he had gazed at the pair—especially at the tall man—a moment. "The waters did not ingulf him after his brutal deed."

The man was indeed Flash Gilmor.

The small officer seemed to be his companion, for the pair stood side by side, looking at the many colored lanterns that were being run to the top of the pole in the center of the plaza or square.

"Oh, for a sword, face to face with you, ruffian!" exclaimed Bentham, and the next moment he turned quickly to the negro.

"Wait here for me, Jupe," he said, and before Jupe could utter a remonstrance he was gone.

"Is de man crazy!" cried the negro, unconsciously speaking aloud and causing several bystanders to notice him. "Hyer me is, not an hour in de city, an' Massa Bob puts off arter de first enemy him sees. Dat's no way to carry out a plan!" and Jupe started off to find the gunner.

Meanwhile Bentham, his blood at the boiling point and rage tugging at his heartstrings, was making his way toward Flash Gilmor and his companion.

"He won't recognize me—I know it," the young gunner was saying to himself. "I am going to settle accounts with him first, and that before dawn."

A minute later he reached Flash Gilmor's side, and jostled him with more spirit than gentility.

Instantly the Southerner turned and demanded an apology in no civil voice.

"This is my apology!" flashed Bentham, and the

back of his hand was laid across Gilmor's flushed face. "I love to strike a coward wherever I find him!"

An oath of rage—an expression of indignation from the little Confederate captain—nothing more.

Gilmor dared not resent the blow.

He realized that a duel would reveal his presence in Nassau to captain Powers—one of the last things to be desired, for the Captain of the Swiftwing knew that he had taken Mowbray's life.

Bentham, after dealing the blow, stepped back and gazed at the murderer.

The little captain stepped forward.

"My friend dare not fight here," he said, addressing the gunner, and sending a quick look at Gilmor. "If you are spoiling for a fight, sir, I can accommodate you in my friend's stead. I am Captain Nugent of the Confederate service."

Bob Bentham threw a look of contempt at the speaker.

"Me fight you?" he exclaimed. "I have no quarrel with a pygmy. Besides, I would not like to pierce the elegant uniform you wear!"

With the last word he turned on his heel and left Gilmor and the Confederate captain to their amazement.

CHAPTER XXII.

CATCHING A TARTAR.

BENTHAM'S blow had been witnessed by but few persons, and the young gunner had disappeared even before those few could realize what had happened.

"Come, Nugent, let us get away from here," said Flash Gilmor, addressing his companion, the Confederate captain. "I would give my right arm if I had been in a position to avenge that cowardly stroke. I know why it was dealt. The man must be a fool if he thinks I cannot penetrate his disguise. This affair does not end here; but, first, let me get out of sight of these staring people."

Gilmor almost dragged Captain Nugent from the spot.

"That man was Bentham, the Yankee gunner, whose shot sunk the Swiftwing," Gilmor said, after the twain had entered the cabin of a vessel lying in the harbor. "I did not recognize him till after he struck; but I am not mistaken. I know what brings him to Nassau. He has found out what happened on board the Foxhound, and he couldn't control himself when he saw me—that's the whole upshot of the matter. I wish I hadn't a certain fear before my eyes. I'd like to fight Bentham."

"Why not accommodate him," said the Confederate. "Powell is gone, you know."

"But Dick Powers still remains. He wants me as

badly as Powell ever did. He will sail day after to-
morrow, thank heaven! Then, I will be at liberty to
fight the Yankee gunner; and, by my soul! I'll run
him through without mercy! You will stand by me,
captain?"

" Draw on me for any assistance desired," was
Nugent's reply; "the drafts will be honored. I would
have forced Bentham into a personal encounter when
he insulted you, if I could have done so without com-
promising your safety, but I dared not, you know."

"Of course; but when the Destroyer puts to sea, I
will be at liberty to pay the several debts I owe certain individuals here," said Gilmor. "I more than
half believe that Captain Powers knows that I am
somewhere in Nassau."

" I am convinced that he does. That window affair
was exceedingly rash."

Gilmor smiled.

" By Jove! I could not help it, captain," he exclaimed. " I was passing along and caught a glimpse
of the two girls through the network of plant leaves.
Curiosity drew me to the window, and I heard Dora's
opinion of Flash Gilmor. When I beheld Norah alone
in the room I felt like telling her that I was still alive
to complete the triumph on which I have set my
heart. She came to the window and put forth her
hand to pluck a delicate flower. I encircled her waist
with my fingers before I could control myself. She
knew me at once, and starting back with a light cry,
she fell to the floor in a swoon. Of course I hurried
away. After that, that spot was no place for me."

" As I have said, your adventure was a risky one.
I am surprised that nothing has grown out of it," the

Confederate captain said. " For some reason or other, the two women are keeping secret your presence here."

Gilmor was silent for a moment, during which time he poured out and drained a glass of wine, which immediately lent a strange glitter to his eyes.

" That little matter we were discussing this afternoon must not fall through, captain," resumed Gilmor.

" No; but doesn't Bentham's arrival complicate matters just a little ?"

" I cannot see how. I will fight him first. After that the Seabird can sail."

" Fix things to suit yourself," smiled Nugent. " I am ready to sail at an hour's notice, but, to tell the truth, Flash, I'd like to carry that Yankee gunner with me."

" On the same vessel that conveys Norah from Nassau ?" ejaculated Gilmor, staring at Nugent. " Would that not be a risky piece of business ?"

" Not at all!" laughed the little Confederate. " A man in irons on board the Seabird could harm no one; but you are determined to fight him first ?"

" Yes! come what may, I will fight him !" and Flash Gilmor leaped to his feet and brought a clinched hand down upon the table between them with a vehemence that shook the glasses and decanters upon it. " If I disarm him and draw some of his blood he shall be yours, captain. I'll not try to kill him unless—unless he plays the tiger and lunges at my heart."

" Where will you fight him ?"

" In the grove on the seashore just beyond the city's limits."

" When ?"

"Any time after the sailing of the Destroyer. I have to wait until Powers has put to sea. I wish that man and his new privateer were at the bottom of the ocean!"

It was thus determined that Flash Gilmor should fight Bentham after the departure of the new and formidable privateer which had been purchased for Powers since his arrival at Nassau.

They went so far as to select the ground and name the time—all this without consulting the Union gunner.

They knew that Bentham would not shrink from the encounter, for he was eager to meet Flash Gilmor, and avenge Mowbray's death.

It was still dark when the two men left the captain's cabin and adjourned to the quarter-deck with a couple of prime cigars.

The sky was overcast, but a delightful breeze blew across the bay, which was well studded with water-craft of all kinds.

Gilmor owed the preservation of his life to Captain Nugent, of the blockade runner Seabird, and his escape from the Foxhound after the killing of Gordon Mowbray.

Fortune or fate favored him, for after rowing hard from the Foxhound until near dawn he was picked up by the Seabird, Captain Nugent, on her way to Nassau.

It happened that Gilmor and the blockade runner were old friends, and the meeting at sea proved mutually agreeable.

The Seabird reached Nassau without accident; but Gilmor was obliged to move about with caution, for shortly after his arrival Captain Powell ran into port, having Nora and Captain Powers of the doomed Swift-wing on board.

Powell did not disturb him, but Powers set to work to get a new ship which, when it had been purchased, he renamed the Destroyer, in accordance with his oath, and got ready for sea.

He commanded a ship superior in build and arma-ment to the Swiftwing and he confidently expected to carry everything before him.

He would avenge the destruction of his first vessel; he would hunt the Avenger down and force her to surrender, or send her with her crew to the depths of the ocean.

Flash Gilmor and his companion, who affected the uniform of a Confederate captain, though only a blockade runner, enjoyed their cigars on the Seabird's quarter-deck for some time without molestation.

All at once Captain Nugent stepped forward and leaned anxiously over the ship's side.

The water lay dark and almost rippleless under the vessel's keel; but it was certain that Nugent's ears had caught a suspicious sound.

There was just light enough on deck to enable Gilmor to see his figure leaning over the railing.

What had startled the captain?

As the minutes wore away, the young Confederate's anxiety increased, until he at last glided to Nugent's side.

At that moment the Seabird's captain turned his face toward him.

"There's a boat down yonder," he said, in the lowest of whispers, which was loud enough to make Gilmor start. "I thought I heard it awhile ago. You can't hear it now; neither can I, because it's directly beneath us."

"What does it mean?" asked Gilmor.

"It's the boat of a spy, of course," was the quick reply in the same tones. "I can make out its outlines in spite of the night. There's only one man in it. Hold—I'll fix him!"

Nugent disappeared, but soon came back, bearing in his hands a long coil of black rope, at one end of which was a slip-loop like the noose of a lasso.

"I'll give the spy a surprise he isn't looking for." He smiled, uncoiling the rope. "We'll just pull him up on deck and inspect him at our leisure."

"Can we do it, captain?"

"Trust to me."

The Confederate leaned over the railing of the ship and looked downward again.

The boat and its occupant were still in the position he had last seen them.

Flash Gilmor held his breath.

A minute later the noose descended from Nugent's hands, and all at once a startled cry broke the stillness of the night.

"I have him, Gilmor! Here! help me pull him up!" exclaimed Nugent.

Flash Gilmor seized the rope, braced himself beside his companion, and both men pulled together.

It was evident that Nugent had lassoed a spy whose resisting powers were rather prodigious.

The two Confederates had no child's task on their hands; but, hand over hand, they gradually drew their capture up the Seabird's side.

"Another foot and we'll see him, Gilmor."

The last word had scarcely left Nugent's tongue, when a dark shape appeared over the top of the ship's railing, and the next instant a huge figure alighted on the deck.

Nugent and Gilmor were almost thrown down by the sudden slackening of the cord.

"Great heaven—a negro!" fell from Gilmor's lips.

"Yes; a black debbil, too, Massa Flash," was the quick retort; and the following instant a tigerish bound carried the sable speaker to the assassin's side.

"Jupe!" he gasped.

"Dat's who I am!"

Before Gilmor could draw a weapon, he was jerked off his feet and hurried to the ship's side.

"Help, Nugent!" pealed from his throat in accents of terror. "The black fiend is going to kill me."

The Confederate captain sprung quickly to Gilmor's rescue, but before he could render any assistance, the young Southerner was pitched headlong into the sea.

An oath burst from Nugent's throat.

"By my soul, you shall pay for that deed!" he exclaimed.

"Mebbe so, Cap'n Nugent," replied the negro, as he wheeled upon him.

The Confederate could not use the sword he had drawn, for the black man leaped upon him, dealt him three blows in blinding succession, and flung him away.

"Dat's what yer git fur lassoin' a darky," ejaculated Jupe. "De next time I guess you'll let him go away without cotchin' 'im."

Jupe sprung toward the railing just as a number of the crew made their appearance on deck.

A rush was made for him, but he lowered himself over the ship's side, dropped into the boat and rowed away.

Captain Nugent had caught a Tartar.

CHAPTER XXIII.

MOVEMENTS OF PERIL.

"WELL, what did you discover, Jupe?" asked Bentham, who was found by the giant negro an hour after the events just recorded.

"Yah, yah?" was the darky's reply, as his eyes twinkled merrily. "You see, Massa Bob, I found a boat at de wharf an' I row out to whar dey tole me Cap'n Nugent's ship lay. I seed two little lights on de quarter, an' I knowed dat Flash Gilmor, an' de cap'n war enjoyin' deir cigars all to demselves. I went closer, till I war right under dem, listenin' to all dat dey war sayin', for dey didn't lower deir voices, but talked as if ole Jupe war away in Norf Caroliny. But all at once, Massa Bob, suffin' like a snake drop ober my shoulders, an' de next minit I war pulled upward like a man when he's hung. Golly, but I war skeered fo' a minit; but den I says to myself: 'Dem two chaps cotch a Tartar in ole Jupe!' an' suah enuff dat's de bery way it turned out, yah, yah, yah! Jes' as I touched de deck Massa Gilmor, de rascal, him say: 'Jupe, by heben!' an' I went fo' him."

"You didn't kill him, Jupe?"

"Guess not, Massa Bob. Ole Jupe pick 'im up an' toss 'im into de sea—dat's all."

"Over the ship's side?"

"Ob course! I didn't carry 'im down an' lay 'im gently in de water. I wouldn't be so keerful wid

such a chap as Flash Gilmor, what shoot ole Mars'
Mowbray. Den I turned on Cap'n Nugent, who war
drawin' his sword. I touched 'im two or free times
wid my fist, an' den toss 'im away."

"Overboard ?"

" No, down de deck. De sailors came up den ; dey
had heard de tussle from below, an' ole Jupe had to
make tracks fo' de boat. Him git away jes' in time,
an' hyer he is, Massa Bob, ready fo' de next job."

Bentham smiled.

" I didn't expect your expedition to terminate thus,
Jupe," he said; "but you couldn't have done other-
wise under the circumstances. What did you hear
Gilmor and the captain say before you were caught ?"

"Dey war talkin' about you, Massa Bob. Dat
Flash Gilmor's bound to fight you arter de Destroyer
sails."

" Oho !" ejaculated the young gunner. "He had
better fight before that event takes place. Well, what
else, Jupe ?"

"From what I heard I calculate dat dey war goin'
ober some plans dey had laid some time afore. Cap'n
Nugent him tell Flash how him will fix up a stateroom
fo' a lady passenger him expects to carry from Nassau
when de Seabird puts to sea."

" His words can have but one meaning," exclaimed
Bentham. "Flash Gilmor is at the bottom of the
whole scheme. Not content with murdering my uncle
he wants to get Norah in his power. She is the expected passenger. Let the rascal do his worst if he
can. Jupe, we must go to work to-night."

"I'se ready, Massa Bob. Jes' work out de plan, an'
let Jupe know what he's to do."

Bentham and his faithful friend were under the roof of a man whom they could trust.

There were a few hearts in Nassau that beat for the Union cause; but the great majority were in sympathy with the Confederacy.

It was through the few that the loyal cruisers were kept posted about the movements of Confederate privateers and blockade runners that arrived at and departed from the wharves.

Bentham had been told by Captain Graham, how and where to find the Union sympathizers, and after Jupe had disposed of Black Tom, Captain Powers' spy, the twain lost no time in reaching the house.

The Unionist received them cordially, and offered them concealment and any assistance that lay in his power.

His sympathies were well known, but he stood so high in the opinions of the British authorities that, up to the night with which we are now dealing, he had not been openly molested.

The Confederacy, however, had dogged his steps with its keenest spies, but he had baffled them all. He was fearless, cunning and cautious, a match for his foes.

This man entered the room shortly after Jupe had finished the narrative of his adventures.

He was a middle-aged person, handsome, robust and tall, and a good-natured smile appeared at the corners of his mouth as he shut the door.

"Jupe is back again," said Bentham, addressing the newcomer.

"So I see," was the response; "but if he did not do better work this time than he did when he handled

Captain Powers' spy I fear he will not be of much service to you, Mr. Bentham."

The young gunner started.

"What has happened?" he asked, betraying some nervousness.

"Black Tom is on board the Destroyer."

Bentham sprung up.

"Golly! didn't I settle dat black spy?" exclaimed Jupe, his distended eyes seemingly on the eve of flying from their sockets.

"You certainly did not," was the answer. "After you stabbed him, you threw him into a hole that yawned before you?"

"Yes, massa."

"Well, that hole led into the cellar of one of the most prominent Southern residents of Nassau. Tom was found shortly afterward, not dead by any means, although in a sad condition. He was able to say that he belonged to the new privateer, Destroyer, and he was conveyed thither. Captain Powers was there when he arrived, and he knows that you are in Nassau."

The sympathizer's last words were addressed to Bentham, whose eyes were filled with astonishment.

"He is hunting me now?" he said. in a voice full of defiance.

"He is in the city. I need not tell you his mission."

The young gunner was silent for a minute.

He saw the deperate situation of affairs.

His presence in Nassau was known to his old rival, Captain Powers, and that before he had seen Norah, to protect whom he had fearlessly entered the lion's den.

The captain of the Destroyer was liable to arrive at the door at any moment; then his daring expedition would end in—smoke!

"As I have told you, I have heard about you many times," said the Unionist, breaking in upon our hero's thoughts. "You are a brave man, Robert Bentham, and the cause we both serve cannot afford to lose you. You must not fall into Dick Powers' hands. As for Norah, I will see that she is protected in spite of Flash Gilmor and the privateer. You must leave Nassau."

"Without seeing Norah—without accomplishing anything? Never!" exclaimed the young gunner.

"Dat's de talk!" put in Jupe. "We'se hyer fo' a purpose, an' all de Captain Powerses in de world ain't goin' to skeer us off."

The Unionist looked serious.

"I regret your determination—not for my sake at all, but wholly for your own," he said, continuing to address Bentham. Captain Powers will not leave a single stone unturned in his search for you. He will make the authorities open my house to him."

"Then we will leave your home," said Bentham. "I do not want to compromise you. No! there are other hiding places in Nassau. I am not wholly unacquainted with the place."

The gunner moved toward the door as he finished, but the Unionist stopped before him.

"I do not fear Dick Powers' hunt—don't think so for a moment," he said, laying his hand on Bentham's arm, and looking him calmly in the eye. "My roof shall shelter you while you stay in Nassau; but when I advised departure I thought I was acting for your good. You will not go?"

" I shall stay !"

Those three words were enough.

The Unionist moved across the room and opened a door of whose existence up to that time the gunner was not aware.

" Dar wasn't a do' dar a minit ago !" ejaculated Jupe, astonished, as the sympathizer motioned them into a room thus displayed. "Dis am a wonderful house, whar de owner kin make do's in a minit in de solid wall."

Having stepped across the mysterious threshold Bentham and the darky found themselves in a small, dimly lighted room, entirely devoid of furniture.

The Unionist next raised a trapdoor in the floor, revealing a dark, cavernous opening, and the head of a flight of steps.

"We will descend," he said to Bentham, who instantly clutched his arm.

"This is flight !" said the young gunner, hesitating —even drawing back.

"It is the avenue to safety," was the answer. " You are still in Nassau ; you are not going to leave it. Follow me !"

Thus answered, Bentham descended the steps at the Unionist's beck, he was in turn followed by Jupe, who entered the underground apartment with many fears.

The trapdoor shut without noise above the party who stood at the foot of the stair in a dark place whose dimensions they could not see.

The Avenger's gunner felt a hand on his arm, and a moment later he was treading a corridor as dark as midnight.

Jupe was stepping at his heels.

This journey terminated at the end of twenty minutes, and the sympathizer led the way up a flight of steps into a room well lighted by a lamp.

Jupe let slip a sigh of relief, but did not speak.

" Powers will never find you here, unless——"

The speaker paused, for a gentle rap sounded on a door at his right.

Stepping lightly across the room, he opened the portal an inch, and Bentham caught a glimpse of a young girl's face.

" Thank heaven for your coming, father!" said a woman's voice. " Three men have been in the garden for an hour."

The Unionist started and turned to Bentham.

" You see how I am watched," he said with a smile.

At that moment a loud knocking startled every one.

" Heavens ! They have discovered all !" gasped the girl.

The young gunner drew his revolver and prepared for a desperate resistance.

CHAPTER XXIV.

HUNTED DOWN.

It was, indeed, a critical moment for Bob Bentham.

The house which they had reached by traversing the underground passage belonged to the Union sympathizer, like the one they had left.

Discovery so soon was an event entirely unlooked-for.

It was more than likely that the three men seen in the garden by the girl during her father's absence were spies in Captain Powers' employ.

The loud knocking still echoed throughout the room when the young gunner stepped forward with drawn revolver.

"Ask who is there," said the Unionist calmly, addressing his daughter.

The young girl went fearlessly to the door.

"Who are you?" she asked.

There was no reply for a moment, but subdued voices told that a number of men were holding a consultation outside.

"They are not our friends—that is certain," said the Unionist, glancing at the gunner, who stood erect with eyes fastened on the door. "If you will go back to the tunnel, I will admit them. You and Jupe can follow the passage back to the other house. It cannot mislead you."

Bentham hesitated.

"Yes, go!" cried the young girl, springing toward him, and laying a white hand on his arm. "For heaven's sake, sir, carry out father's instructions. We must let the authorities search the house."

"Ain't you going to open the door?" assailed the ears of all before Bentham could reply.

"Yes, sir," said the daughter, then adding to Bentham, in a low tone: "To the tunnel—quick! You have not a moment to lose!"

The young gunner was about to obey despite his inclinations, which were to stay and fight it out with the men on the outside, when a heavy body fell against the door and a loud voice exclaimed:

"We can't parley all night. Business is business. The Yankee gunner shall not escape us!"

"No!" grated Bentham; "the Yankee gunner will stay and show his hand. Here, Jupe, stand ready to give these fellows a warm reception when they come in."

The giant negro sprung forward with an ejaculation of eagerness, while the cheeks of the Unionist and his daughter grew pale.

The next moment the door was heavily thumped the second time, the lock gave way, and, as it flew open, a tall, heavily-bearded and dark-faced man fell headlong into the room.

Others promptly succeeded him until, in a moment, six had entered.

"We want that infamous Yankee gunner!" cried the head intruder, as he faced the Unionist. "We are Confederate sailors, and——"

"I am here!" interrupted Bentham, presenting his revolver so near the ruffian's face that he started back with surprise. "If you seek the chief gunner of the United States cruiser Avenger, you need go no further."

"Great heavens! Bob Bentham himself!"

The gunner smiled.

"Dat's jes' who he am," put in Jupe, who faced the surprised group like a lion about to spring. "I'se heart an' soul wid Massa Bob whatever he does; so if you men want 'im, hyer he is."

"You surrender, of course, Mr. Bentham," said the leader of the hunters, throwing a quick glance through his party as if to call the gunner's attention to its superiority. "Our orders are to secure you."

A smile curled Bentham's lips.

"Who sent you out?" he asked.

"Captain Powers, of the Destroyer."

"I thought so. Tell Captain Powers that I do not surrender to his agents."

"Then——"

"Yes, sir, I resist!" was the thrilling interruption; and the revolver was suddenly lifted and thrust into the faces of the group. "Gentlemen, I do not desire bloodshed, but I am not your prisoner. The man who lifts a hand or moves falls dead where he stands!"

"Dat's de talk dat means sumffin'," cried Jupe. "Gemmen, Massa Bentham hab got more shoot in dem eyes of his'n den any oder man in Nassau."

Dark looks fell upon the negro from the eyes of the Confederate band, but no one replied to his words.

"We were not to shed blood," said the leader, addressing Bentham. "You have the drop on us, and a human life should be valued above all things. About face, boys. We will report to the captain."

The brawny sailors turned away with growls of mingled disappointment and rage, but the fierce looks that they darted at Bentham told them that the drama had not been played through.

"I will not say good-night," said the leader, as he paused on the threshold and turned to the little group that occupied the room. "We may meet again before morning. I may add that Captain Powers is determined to carry out his plans. Your servant's knife, Mr. Bentham, failed to do its work thoroughly."

Then, before any one could reply, he turned away, and the sympathizer's daughter shut the door behind the gang.

For a moment after this unexpected riddance nobody spoke.

The situation seemed to fall like a pall over all.

What was to be done?

"Golly! I war itchin' to gib dat head Confed a thumpin'!" exclaimed Jupe, showing his sable fists. "Didn't I know 'im, de ole rapscallion? He war Jasper Jones, de man what cheated Massa Mowbray outen six niggers befo' de wah. I come mighty near bein' one ob dem coons, an' now I'd like to pulverize 'im fo' dat trick. Dey'll come back—no mistake 'bout dat."

"That is true, Jupe," said the girl. "Those men have not gone off for good. Father, Mr. Bentham must not be here when they return."

"I will not be," was the gunner's quick response. "As I have said, I do not wish to compromise you. I should have retired to the tunnel at your suggestion, my friend, but those fellows made my blood flow like molten lava through my veins, and——"

"There!" was the quiet interruption, and the sympathizer even smiled as he spoke. "I fear not for myself. You see those men didn't have anything like a search warrant from the English authorities here. We should have been warned in ample time if they had. That is why they took me by surprise. I am convinced that they will come again determined to secure you."

"They will subject your daughter and yourself to insult if I am not found."

"They dare not go that far; and nobody knows that better than Captain Dick Powers," was the response. "They will search the house. I shall not resist, for reasons best known to myself. They might even discover the tunnel."

"Hark!" said the girl.

The Unionist bounded instantly toward the room into which Bentham and Jupe had lately emerged from the subterranean passage.

The gunner saw him stoop and listen intently with one ear near the floor.

"Captain Powers has two bands on the lookout for you, Bentham," he said, rising suddenly and facing the anxious gunner. "The other one has discovered the tunnel. I hear them in it now."

"There must be a traitor somewhere," said Bentham.

The Unionist said nothing; but his brows darkened.

"Follow my instructions this time and ask no questions," he said in hurried but serious tones to Bentham. "It is a good thing that you did not take to the tunnel awhile ago."

"But you——"

" I tell you that Jennie and I are able to take care of ourselves. Follow me—no questions, mind you. I will not let you stay here another moment. Come."

He led the way across the room.

" Go with father," said the girl imploringly to the young gunner. " He will direct you to a house which all the Confederates in Nassau dare not enter without authority."

In another minute Bentham and Jupe had left the house, and stood in the dark garden behind it.

" I am sure that the coast is clear," whispered the Unionist. " Follow this path—you see it ?"

" Yes."

" It will lead you to a narrow street. Take to the right and count the houses on your left hand. At the tenth one stop, look behind you carefully, then enter the yard and knock thrice at the door. It will be opened by a young woman to whom you will say : 'We come from Throxton,' as you enter. You will then be safe. Go! I will meet you again. Recollect that you have not yet fought Flash Gilmor, and that the Destroyer may sail the high seas under the Stars and Stripes, and not with the new flag at her peak."

A pressure of hands followed the last words, and Bentham and his faithful companion soon found themselves traversing the gloomy street which they found at the foot of the Unionist's garden.

We may imagine the eagerness with which the fearless young gunner counted the houses at his left.

In front of the tenth one they halted according to the Unionist's instructions, and having made sure that they were not observed, Bentham went forward and gave the three raps.

Almost immediately the door was opened by a young girl of exceeding loveliness, to whom the gunner bowed with his foot on the threshold.

" We come from Throxton," he said.

There was a low exclamation of assent, and as the door was still held open Jupe went forward.

As the door closed behind them Bentham caught sight of a female figure on a sofa, and a minute afterward a young lady stood before him.

" Norah !" cried the young man, starting back..

" Robert !" was the response.

" Wal, ef it tain't de young missus may I neber see ole Caroliny any mo' !" ejaculated Jupe.

It was a strange, unexpected meeting.

For a moment the lovers stood face to face, then their hands and lips met.

The girl who had opened the door looked wonderingly on.

" This is Mr. Bentham, the Yankee gunner, Dora," said Norah, turning to Captain Powell's niece. " I am sure he is a hunted man, and——"

" He is safe here !" she said calmly.

CHAPTER XXV.

CAPTAIN POWERS' NEW SPY.

CAPTAIN POWERS was determined to unearth Bob in Nassau.

He had secured a new vessel, which was to more than take the place of the Swiftwing on the seas.

This ship, called the Destroyer, as we have already informed the reader, lay at the wharf almost ready for sea.

Her sides were plated, her smokestack and decks well protected, and she carried the best guns that money could procure.

This was the vessel destined by her captain to become mistress of the seas—overcome the Avenger, and sink her beneath the waves that now rolled restlessly over the Swiftwing.

Powers had recruited a crew on whom he could depend.

It consisted of men who had seen some desperate service, and who were ready to engage in any enterprise that offered itself.

They all knew the man under whom they had enlisted, for Dick Powers had a reputation for daring which lifted him high in the estimation of thousands.

A part of this crew were the men who had driven Bentham and Jupe from the Union sympathizer's house, forcing them to take refuge elsewhere.

Another portion of the band entered the other house

and by diligent searching discovered the tunnel, into which they plunged, hoping to overtake the gunner.

"Foiled in their attempts to capture Bentham, the sailors went back to Powers with their report.

He listened with flashing eyes and clinched teeth.

"So he escaped you, eh?" he said. "You found him, but he got away. Why didn't you set a watch on the house when you left? Never mind! he shall not escape me. I will make Nassau the warmest place he was ever in. I will run him to earth, for I do not intend to leave port until I can carry him with me ironed in the Destroyer's hold."

This was a resolve which Captain Powers determined to carry out.

He forgot in his rage to send the sailors back to the trail, but descended to his cabin, where a giant negro lay on a pallet on the floor.

"Wal, Marse Powers, did ye cotch de rascal?" asked the black, as he turned and looked at the privateer.

"Not yet, Tom."

"Him got clear off, eh?"

"For awhile—that is all."

"An' Jupe de debbil wid 'im?"

"Yes."

The wounded negro grated his teeth.

"I'se gwine to die, Marse Powers, but I wants to feel Jasper's throat first," was hissed from between the darky's teeth. "Jes' let me git my black claws dar, an' I'll cross de riber widout a murmur. Dar's a million knives stickin' in my back dis blessed minute, but it won't be fo' long, Marse Powers—not fo' long. Ole Tom's nigh de riber now, bery nigh; but him want to clutch Jupe's throat afo' he crosses."

It was evident that the spy was near his end, for a strange rattling in his throat followed the last word.

Captain Powers bestowed another glance upon him and left the cabin—left the man who had served him faithfully to die alone.

Ten minutes later the privateersman was in Nassau.

He was unattended and hurried down the darkened streets as if eager to reach a certain point within a given time.

"Nassau isn't large enough to afford him a hiding place!" he muttered, his thoughts returning to his enemy. "If this city was London, he should not escape me. My men failed, and that when they stood face to face with him, but I will not. I want to pay him back for that sword-thrust on the banks of Cape Fear. By heavens, he shall discover that I pay my debts with the interest of vengeance!"

A short distance further on Powers knocked at the door of a house that stood back from the street, with a garden in front of it.

There were no lights about the premises to show that they were inhabited; but this did not deter the captain.

His raps had scarcely ceased when the door was opened—just wide enough to admit a man—and he sprung inside.

"Captain Powers!" exclaimed a voice as the privateersman halted beyond the threshold.

"It is I, Peter. Where is Mardo?"

The man who confronted the visitor in the dimly lighted and almost bare room disappeared for a moment to usher in a dark-skinned, snake-eyed man who had the movements of a serpent.

He was a Malay—this Mardo—a born spy and devil. He knew every hole and corner of Nassau, and the creese that he carried at his belt had doubtless taken the life of more than one man while he served different masters.

He instantly recognized Powers, whom he approached and touched with a thug's smile.

" Does the captain want Mardo ?" he inquired.

" I do," was the reply, as Powers made a sign for the person who had admitted him to retire, which sign was obeyed.

He was alone with the Malay, who had been brought to Nassau five years previous to our story by a sea captain who wanted a rival hunted down.

We need not record what passed between the pair in that old house, so dark outside and so dimly lighted within.

Suffice to say that half an hour later a crouching figure went through the Union sympathizer's garden like a bloodhound on the trail.

Escape a Malay spy if you can !

The man who stood in the old house waiting impatiently for the spy's return was Captain Dick Powers.

He was trusting his sailors no longer ; but had put all his dependence in one man whose eyes seemingly could look through a stone wall

The crouching Malay was on the right trail.

He knew that two men had crossed the garden and gained the street beyond, but there his trail seemed to end. Still he did not despair !

He had the perseverance of the born sleuth ; therefore he kept on.

With the noiseless tread of the panther he crept from house to house, listening under the window sills, and among the trees which fronted nearly all the residences.

His journey took him to Captain Powell's house.

He crouched at one of the windows.

Why did he start, and what made his eyes twinkle so maliciously?

Had the crawling Malay spy discovered anything?

One thing is certain—that his trail ended here.

He listened beneath no more windows, but glided away and soon disappeared.

If the Malay had gcod eyes, his ears were also excellent.

When close to the old house where Captain Powers awaited him, he stopped and listened.

Had he been followed?

At any rate, after listening awhile he drew his creese and stepped behind a tree near by.

There he stood waiting for the person approaching to come up.

That individual did not seem willing to oblige Mardo, for all at once the footsteps ceased; they sounded again a moment later, but going back.

"Spy 'fraid to come on!" growled the Malay, disappointedly. "Santissima! Mardo will find him if him afraid to meet Mardo."

So saying the yellow leopard turned and went back after the person who had evidently been following him.

The Malay's feet gave forth no sound as eager bounds sent him swiftly forward.

He still carried the naked creese in his right hand—ready to bury it in the back of his victim.

At last his eyes caught sight of the person who had tracked him.

The man was moving toward Captain Powell's house, wholly oblivious of the terrible danger that threatened him.

All at once with a leap not unlike the airy spring of the jaguar, Mardo went through the air, and alighted on the shoulders of the spy.

There was an exclamation of horror uttered in a thick voice, and the person attacked whirled while it still sounded.

" Look heah, you mean spy, I'se Jupe !" and a black hand clutched the Malay's uplifted arm before it could drive the creese home.

Mardo uttered an oath of madness !

He attempted to free himself, but the giant negro was too quick for him.

If the Malay possessed the agility of a cat, the black had the strength of a lion, and coupled to it was the rage of a wounded king of beasts.

How the eyes of the two spies glittered as they glared at one another in the light that came from a window near by !

" You no nigger dis time !" said Jupe, unable to decide his assailant's nationality. " But I know what you'se arter, all de same. Want Massa Bob, eh ? Cap'n Powers sent you, mebbe."

At the mention of the privateer's name the Malay started, and again attempted to use his knife ; but the black prevented.

" You go see Massa Bob, dat's sartin," continued Jupe, whose grip could not be shaken loose. " Him anxious to see what kind ob spies Cap'n Dick find in

Nassau. Heah, no squirmin' fo' dis chile kin hold you fast till Gabrul blow his horn, if him wants to."

While the last sentence was falling from the darky's tongue he was walking rapidly away, carrying Mardo with him, despite his struggles, which momentarily grew fainter, for one of the sable hands, which had the pressing power of a vice, was at his throat, almost as delicate as a woman's.

A few steps brought Jupe and his prisoner to Captain Powell's house.

He sprung toward it—and struck the door three times with his foot.

A light cry from the lips of a woman was heard, as Jupe strode through the open door.

"Heavens! it is Mardo the Malay!" exclaimed Dora.

"Dis yaller dog prowlin' round too promiscuously!" answered Jupe, surveying the startled trio whom he confronted—Bentham and the two women. "Him spring on Jupe like a catamount; but dis chile too quick fo' him. I'll fix him now!"

At that instant the darky raised Mardo as high above his head as his long sable arms would elevate him.

The spy almost touched the ceiling.

Fire flashed from Jupe's eyes.

"Him no git away like Black Tom did!" he grated.

Bentham saw the negro's intention, and bounded forward to prevent the deed about to be committed.

"Hold Jupe!" he exclaimed. "No crime in this house!"

"No—no! Massa Bob. Dis snake shan't crawl after you any mo'!" replied Jupe, retreating from before the young gunner.

The next moment the negro seemed to increase several inches in stature, and all at once Mardo the Malay was thrown upon the floor with a force great enough to break every bone in his body.

"Now let de yaller serpint crawl if he kin!" exclaimed Jupe, casting a look of triumph upon the privateer's spy, who lay on the floor apparently dead, but with his knife, the deadly creese, still clutched in his right hand.

The two women started back with blanched faces.

"You have killed him, Jupe!" exclaimed Bentham.

"Dat seems to be a fact, Massa Bob," was the giant's answer, as he grinned. "Wonder what Cap'n Dick 'd say ef he could look in heah an' see de Malay man on de flo'—dead?"

If Jupe had failed to finish the captain's first spy, Black Tom, he had made sure work of the second.

Mardo the Malay was dead, killed by that crushing descent to the floor from the hands of his captor.

After years of spying the yellow leopard had met his match, and Jupe had again saved Bentham's life.

If Captain Powers would secure his rival, the loyal young gunner, he must first rid the world of Jupe, who seemed destined to baffle him on every occasion.

Ah! he may wait in the little old house for his yellow spy.

He would never come again.

CHAPTER XXVI.

CAPTAIN POWELL BOBS UP SERENELY.

WHILE the events that occupy the two last chapters were transpiring in Nassau, a boat rowed by two men was approaching the city.

One of the men was Foulweather Tom, late pilot of the Foxhound ; the other was well dressed, like a ship's master, but his garments had at one time been saturated with water, as could easily be seen.

He rowed with his companion, and their strokes sent the boat swiftly through the water.

"We're getting in, Tom," the well-dressed man said to his comrade. "A few more strokes will take us to the dock. The Foxhound's at the bottom of the sea. She did not do that accursed Yankee ship any good. They didn't hoist their flag over her. By Jove! I hated to blow the old ship up ; but I was bound to stick to my word. They think I went to pieces with the bark, no doubt, therefore they didn't hunt for me long. Nobody saw me drop into the sea after I started the fuse that let the hammer fall on the torpedo's cap after it had burned a certain distance. They'll be surprised when they learn that Captain Powell is still engaged in his old business. I'll have a new ship soon, Tom, and over my cabin door I'll write the words you used to see on board the Foxhound: 'This ship will never be taken by the enemy.'"

The pilot looked in Powell's face.

"Will there be a torpedo in the new ship's hold, cap'n?" he asked.

Powell smiled grimly.

"I wouldn't go to sea without one," he answered. "But look yonder, Tom—the lights of Nassau!"

The blockade runner pointed to the many lights of the island city which were reflected in the water like myriads of stars.

The pilot, whose escape from the Foxhound had been more miraculous than Powell's, looked ahead, but said nothing.

He was evidently thinking of the terrible torpedo which would be placed in the hold of the new blockade runner.

Ralph Powell had clambered over his ship's side after lighting the fuse which was to destroy her.

He swam rapidly away, and was some distance from the bark when the awful explosion took place, and consequently out of harm's way.

Spars, timbers, and pieces of iron filled the air everywhere for a moment, and then fell like a shower into the sea.

He had survived the destruction of his ship!

By and by he reached shore, where he was subsequently joined by Foulweather Tom.

Mutual congratulations followed over their escape, and fortune sent a boat to take them from the scene.

The blockade runner was saved to the Confederacy, and he would yet bring it succor time and again from across the seas.

The little boat and its occupants were rapidly nearing Nassau.

The master of the Foxhound was eager to set foot on shore again.

His desire increased as the boat shot over the water almost noiselessly. He could hardly restrain himself.

The boat was passing under the bows of a vessel that lay at anchor in the bay when loud voices were heard, and a heavy body fell into the water.

"That was a man, cap'n," said Tom. "Shiver my toplights! if he fell into the sea of his own accord. Didn't you hear a tusslin' on deck jes' before he hit the water?"

"Let us help him," said Powell, for the person who had fallen into the bay was struggling with the waves a short distance away.

The boat was instantly put about, and rapidly approached the unfortunate man.

"There he is, cap'n! He's makin' for the bark!" exclaimed Jack, whose keen eyes had caught sight of a human being swimming toward a vessel.

"I see him! Pull away, Tom! He must be picked up!"

The person in the water did not seem very anxious to be rescued, for, instead of waiting for the boat, he was putting forth every effort to gain the vessel over whose sides he had fallen.

He was baffled, however, for the strong arms of Powell and his sailor sent the boat between him and the vessel, and he suddenly found himself headed off.

"We're here to save you!" said the blockade runner, leaning forward and clutching the man's shoulder. "We don't belong to your ship—that's a fact—but—Great heavens! it is Flash Gilmor!"

At that selfsame moment a cry of recognition rang from the throat of the man in the water.

"Captain Powell!"

"It's nobody else," was the response, and the speaker's clutch tightened on Gilmor's shoulder. "I'm willing to lose the Foxhound for the chance of finding you again. Fortune favored you the night you escaped after killing Mowbray; but Nemesis has thrown you into my hands. Here, Jack, help me pull this assassin in!"

Flash Gilmor would have resisted if strength would have saved him; but he was completely in the power of the men in the boat.

He was pulled in by brute force, for he did not assist himself in any way, and as he was placed on the bottom of the boat, Powell and the pilot took up the oars again, and sent the craft lying from the spot.

Flash Gilmor thus fell into the hands of the man whom he most dreaded—the man on board whose ship he had committed a most brutal murder.

He knew that Mowbray and Powell were old friends at the time of the former's death, and, therefore, he could expect no mercy at the captain's hands.

For several minutes he lay silent and sullen in the boat, glaring at his captors, but especially at Powell, with the smothered rage of a thwarted tiger.

"I would like to know by what authority you take me to Nassau?" he said sullenly.

The blockade runner smiled.

"The authority that vengeance bestows, of course," the captain answered. "Froth at the mouth, and curse Powell and fate as you please, Flash Gilmor. I was Mowbray's friend. I have a right to avenge his death. Nobody saw you commit the crime. You would set up the plea of self-defense; but a court will never hear you."

"What do you threaten?" asked Gilmor.

"Death—something villains of your stripe never contemplate without shuddering."

Gilmor said nothing, but watched Powell with the glaring eyes of a ruffian.

"It was all for the girl—Norah," continued Powell. "The guardian first—the ward next. Having killed one, you would more than kill the other. But your course is run. This night is your last on earth. I will kill you, unless the devil himself comes to your relief and takes you from my grasp."

Flash Gilmor nursed his rage in silence; and the boat soon lay alongside the dock.

"Where are you about to take me?" demanded Gilmor, when they had disembarked at a secluded wharf.

The neighborhood was dark and deserted, and Flash saw that his captor would do pretty much as he pleased without great fear of interruption.

"You will see presently," returned Powell, in stern tones.

"Do you mean to murder me?" Gilmor said, in depressed accents.

"I mean to kill you," was the reply.

"That's the same thing."

"No; I shall give you a chance for your life. I will strike no man down in cold blood."

"A duel?" said Flash, eagerly catching at the faint hope conveyed by Powell's words, as a drowning man grasps at a straw.

"You have said it; yes."

"You are generous. I accept the issue with pleasure," said Gilmor, who was an expert swordsman and a crack shot.

"You fancy you may escape, eh ?"

"While there's life there's hope," replied Flash, "and I wish to live as well as any other man."

"I dare say ; but you flatter yourself in this case. You cannot escape me."

"At least I shall be able to defend my life. I ask no more than that of any man," said Gilmor defiantly.

During this brief conversation they had been rapidly making their way toward one end of the city, not very far removed from the docks.

"Here, Tom, we turn down this street," said Powell to his pilot.

The party left the deserted thoroughfare through which they had passed from the wharf and entered a narrow street lined with marine junk shops, ship chandlery stores, with here and there a low dram-shop.

The place seemed filled with a saline odor quite in keeping with its mercantile character.

Many of the stores were still open and the second-hand wares exposed for sale.

Everything, from a needle for sewing canvas to an old iron cannon, seemed to be offered at a price phenomenal for its cheapness.

Of clothing there was an abundance, and Jack could fill his slop bag without any great loss of time in the choosing.

Rough blue jackets, with mother-of-pearl buttons, and oilskin hats seemed to predominate.

The windows were filled with a heterogeneous mass of rubbish which had evidently once seen efficient use, and had been parted with by the original owners when they got hard pressed.

There were pawnshops also, dark and dingy looking

places, huddled against their neighbors in a deprecating way, as though apologizing for the necessity of their presence.

The street was filled with sailors in all stages of inebriety, and the dramshops aforesaid were crowded by blockade runners who had not yet parted with their last coin.

Lights flashed through these grimy, smoky dens, and strains of music, such as it was, floated into the purer atmosphere outside.

These scenes were familiar to the three men who moved and elbowed their way through the street.

Fifty pairs of eyes recognized Captain Powell and his pilot, and their salutations and remarks proved that these two were heroes to the nomadic denizens of sailor town.

Had the blockade runner been in the mood and given the word a dozen pair of horny hands would have made an end of Flash Gilmor then and there, without the least ceremony or an inquiry as to the justification of such a lawless act.

And Gilmor knew it, too, though he had no fear of such a result.

He knew that Powell was incapable of treachery.

He had passed his word that the issue was to take the form of a duel, and his word was his bond, as everybody acquainted with the blockade runner knew.

From this marine thoroughfare they passed to another street of much quieter aspect.

Here were shipping offices and small warehouses, all closed for the day.

After walking for some distance down the street the trio drew up before a house well fronted with trees.

It was a large, two-story building, and the only light visible inside came from one of the lower windows.

The men were admitted in response to a knock from Powell.

"We go upstairs, Flash," said the blockade runner, leading the way to a flight of steps almost directly ahead.

Gilmor did not appear to be a prisoner any longer.

He seemed to know what was upstairs, for he went up the steps with much eagerness visible in his eyes.

The trio had entered a building in which scores of men then serving in the Confederate navy had taken their first lessons in swordsmanship.

The room that awaited them on the second floor extended the entire length of the building.

It was dimly lighted, but Powell soon increased the light, revealing a number of sword-racks, well supplied with blades of all kinds. Some revolvers were also visible.

"You know the place, I see—you have been here before," said the blockade runner, noticing the rapid glance of recognition which Flash Gilmor sent round the room.

"The old place has a familiar look," was the reply; "but I believe we came here for a purpose."

"Yes—to fight! Select your weapon."

Did a gleam of satisfaction light up Powell's eyes when he saw Gilmor step toward a case containing some revolvers?

If so, it soon disappeared, for, instead of removing a revolver from the case, Gilmor took a splendid sword from the rack.

"I am ready," he said, whirling upon Powell with the air of a duellist sure of his man.

Captain Powers seized a weapon similar to that secured by his antagonist, and then the two men stood face to face.

" Tom, stand by the door. This is to be a fight to the death. Should I be defeated it is my command that this man may depart unmolested. You understand ?"

" Ay, ay, captain ; it shall be as you say," said the pilot, taking up his station.

" You heard what I said, Flash Gilmor. You are at liberty to go if you best me in this affair. But I don't think you will have the chance to avail yourself of my offer, for as I have already told you, I have made up my mind to kill you, and I mean every word of it, be you the devil himself at the sword.

Gilmor simply smiled.

He felt easy in mind over the result, but he was yet to learn something new at the science he fancied himself the master of.

Flash Gilmor was no coward, and in the present instance did not think he would have to sell his life dearly.

He had made up his mind to run Powell through the body.

CHAPTER XXVII.

THE DUEL TO THE DEATH.

For a breathless moment the duellists stood face to face.

The pilot was the only spectator.

"Are you ready?" asked the blockade runner.

"I am ready!"

"Then at it we go. Look out!"

The next instant blade encountered blade.

From the first the combat was hot.

Flash Gilmor fought with the science of an experienced swordsman, but Powell's thrusts, blows and strokes came so thick and fast, and were so skillfully managed, that Gilmor was forced to recoil.

The blockade runner seemed to be transformed into a veritable devil incarnate with the weapon.

His blade writhed upon that of his adversary like a squirming snake.

No one but such an expert as Gilmor could have withstood him five minutes.

He would have beaten down their guard and pierced them in the twinkling of an eye.

That Gilmor was surprised and discomfited by the discovery that his opponent was a master at the art goes without saying.

It was a perfect revelation to him, and the contest assumed a graver aspect than he could have suspected.

Powell was strong, of great endurance, with nerves

and muscles of steel, and far more flexible than any one would have supposed in a man of his build; and furthermore he was desperately in earnest.

Mowbray's murderer ground his teeth and parried as best he could the strokes of his antagonist.

"I never saw the captain fight that way before," muttered Tom. "He must be losing his head."

No; Captain Powell was bound to kill his antagonist—that was all.

Gilmor had all he could do to maintain a successful defense without attempting to take the initiative himself.

He was soon wounded on his sword arm, again on his wrist.

Then the captain's sword point reached his right cheek, slightly drawing blood.

Gilmor began to lose his coolness by degrees; the contest was too one-sided to suit his views.

He felt that he had better make a desperate effort, than to be reduced by slow degrees, even if he paid for it with his life.

In a word he thought it was better to be struck, so to speak, by the tiger's paw than to be worried to death piecemeal by jackals.

And so steadying himself he began new tactics, and for awhile the contest took on an aspect more favorable to himself.

Powell seemed to be less skillful at defense than attack.

Gilmor perceived his advantage and smiled that old dangerous smile which had preceded the murder of Gordon Mowbray.

Powell slowly retreated, step by step, and the flash

of the weapons took on the gleam of fire under the flickering gaslights.

Foulweather Tom began to have misgivings as to the issue, and his mahogany-hued hands worked nervously as he watched the deadly encounter.

A quick cut of Gilmor's wounded Powell in his sword hand.

Then like a tiger who has tasted blood he quickly resumed his savage attack, and Flash found the tables turned on himself again.

" What! can't I avenge Mowbray ?"

The answer was a defiant look.

Powell's attack now became actually irresistible.

Flash was forced almost to the wall; he could not withstand such a terrible assault.

" You see I have you, assassin !" cried the blockade runner. " Tom and I will be the only persons to leave this room alive."

At that instant Gilmor's sword was beaten from his hand.

He was at Powell's mercy.

Did the victor spare ?

No!

He leaped at his enemy, raising the heavy sword like a saber, and with two tremendous blows, that would have cloven a casque, cut him down !

Powell would have followed the strokes with others as Gilmor reeled away, cut to the death, if the pilot had not thrown himself between the two men regardless of the captain's intentions.

Not a single cry had been driven from Gilmor's throat by the brutal blow.

A gasp parted his lips as he struck the floor—nothing more.

He was dead—and Gordon Mowbray was avenged!

Powell gazed for a moment at his victim. It was a cold, unpitying look.

"He's done for, Tom," he said, turning to the sailor. "Flash didn't think I could use a sword—ha! ha!" And with his triumphant cry echoing in the room the captain and his pilot went down the stair.

CHAPTER XXVIII.

IN WHICH CAPTAIN POWERS COMES TO GRIEF.

THE blockade runner hastened toward his own house.

He was now alone, for he dismissed the pilot with a few gold pieces on the street, and Foulweather Tom had already disappeared.

"The two girls don't expect me to-night," he said to himself. "I wonder how they get along together. Dora will be shocked to hear that the Foxhound is at the bottom of the sea; but her eyes will grow bright again when I tell her that I will soon command on the quarter-deck of another ship as swift and as stanch."

He was near his residence when these words dropped from his lips.

"Captain Powell! by my soul!"

The blockade runner paused and turned.

A few feet away a man stood staring at him as though he were a specter.

"Powers! ah! we meet again!" said the blockade runner, advancing upon the person who had just spoken his name in accents of astonishment.

"Back already, captain?" ejaculated Powers, for the man was the captain of the new privateer, Destroyer. "Have the Yankee cruisers forced you back into port?"

Powell's brows darkened.

" Worse than that," he grated. " The Foxhound is mine no more."

" Surrendered, eh ?"

" No! the torpedo did the work. That Yankee gunner riddled me first. He shoots like a wizard, Powers."

Dick Powers laughed more than half triumphantly as he touched the blockade runner's arm.

" You have reached Nassau in the nick of time," he said. " Bentham is here."

" In Nassau ?"

" In Nassau !"

" Impossible !"

" It is true. He has outwitted me thus far. I even put Mardo on his track, but the Malay never came back to report. He is here for a purpose."

" Of course," said Powell significantly. " I know him for a man of nerve, but I did not think he'd venture into Nassau. So he has beaten you?"

" Yes."

" He shall not escape me. When do you sail ?"

" I can put off at any time."

" But you had a time set for departure ?"

" Yes; day after to-morrow."

" You can leave then, for by that time I will have found Bentham."

" If we put our heads together, he can't elude us long."

Powell fixed his eyes on Powers as the latter spoke.

The two men had never been the best of friends.

The blockade runner probably recalled their last words on board the Foxhound, spoken shortly after Powers' interview with Norah.

He was not going to ally himself with the privateersman in a hunt after the young gunner.

If he had a score to settle with Bentham he would if possible unearth the man himself, and in his own way.

Powers must conduct his own operations as he had begun, entirely on his own responsibility.

Powers seemed to understand that the blockade runner did not want his company, and a defiant light at once gleamed in his eyes.

"We hunt him separately, then, and may the best man win," he said to Powell. "How is Norah getting along? You know I take a great interest in the young lady."

"I cannot answer you. I have not been home," was the reply. "Yes, I know you pretend to think a great deal of her. I believe you lately swore in her presence that you would make her your wife one of these days."

"I did. Ah! you overheard me. I had forgotten."

"And you expect to keep your word?"

"I do."

"Well, you'll fail."

For a moment Powers did not reply.

He seemed to be curbing the rage that was fast getting the better of him.

"You will try and prevent it then?" he said.

"I will."

"We shall see. We serve the same flag; but I don't think we will ever be friends, Powell."

"Never!"

"So be it."

"Captain Powers, you once told Norah that you

would avenge Mowbray's death. You will never do that!"

" Why not?"

" It has been avenged."

The captain of the Destroyer recoiled.

" You have found Flash Gilmor?" he said, in strange tones, as he stared into Powell's face.

"Fate brought us together."

"And you have killed him?"

" Yes."

" Tom and I escorted him to the sword-room in the naval building on Queen Street. I gave him an even chance for his life."

" You did?"

" I did, sir."

" This is astonishing. Why, Flash Gilmor was an expert with both sword and pistol."

" That may be. Indeed, I admit he showed himself a formidable opponent. But I have proved myself his superior with the weapon he chose."

" You allowed him the choice also?"

"Assuredly. I stood in the light of the challenging party, for I forced the issue, and therefore he had the right to select the weapons."

" You were extremely obliging," said Powers, who seemed amazed at what he heard. " Had I been in your place, with such a man at my mercy, I should have allowed him scant courtesy. He killed Gordon Mowbray in cold blood. The old man had not the ghost of a show that fatal morning, if what you told me is true. By that act Flash Gilmor forfeited every right to consideration. You should have killed him as you would a rat—without the least mercy."

"It is not in my nature to do that with any man, be the provocation what it may."

"I presume you will kill me, too, if I persist in loving Norah?" said Powers with a sneer.

"I have nothing to do with your love for the girl. But if you persecute her I will defend and protect her against you."

"Indeed," said Powers coolly.

"Ay, indeed. If you mean the girl well you will conduct your suit on gentle lines. I fancy, however, that you will not succeed."

"And why not, pray?"

"Because it is apparent she does not like you."

"I will overcome that objection."

"There is another obstacle that you will not so easily dispose of."

"Bentham?"

"Ay; unless I am blind in such matters, Norah loves the Yankee gunner."

"I shall fix him, never fear, unless you perform that pleasing duty for me."

"Never mind what I propose to do about Bentham. It is my own affair. All I have to say is to repeat my warning in respect to Norah. She is my guest, or rather my niece's. Leave her alone, Captain Powers, or take the consequences."

"I intend to. You have no right to act as that girl's guardian. If you are championing her cause for a certain purpose, I am ready to enter the lists and tilt for her heart. Let us begin here. There can never be peace between us. Draw!"

Powers stepped back a pace and whipped out the sword he carried at his side.

He did not see that the blockade runner was unarmed; rage blinded him.

Powell's lips met sternly as he executed a rapid stride forward.

"I am unarmed, sir, except with nature's weapons," he said, clutching Powers' right arm. "If I had a dozen swords, I would not fight you here!"

"By Jove! you shall!"

"That is your emptiest boast!" was the cool rejoinder. "I say I will not, so that ends the matter for the present!"

"It does not, I say. You shall fight me. I will lay my sword across your face."

He broke away from Powell's grasp as he uttered the last words, and raised the sword to accomplish his resolve.

The blockade runner leaped at him, knocked the weapon aside and dealt him a stunning blow in the face.

The captain of the Destroyer staggered back, lost his footing, and fell against the door of one of the houses.

It opened like magic and engulfed him, much to Powell's surprise.

"Well, I'll be jiggered!" he exclaimed. "That's Throxton's house, and I believe he's a stanch Unionist, so I don't envy Powers' reception."

His own house was in the same street and only a few paces distant.

He knocked at the door and Dora answered his summons.

She greeted him gladly, but with evident surprise.

"You have been driven back," she said.

" Worse," he answered.

" Worse ?"

" Yes.   The Foxhound is gone."

" Captured ?"

" No—she lies in sixteen fathoms of water off the island of Eleuthera, in the Providence Channel."

" Sunk by Yankee shot ?"

" No ; disabled, but not sunk by Yankee shot. I destroyed her myself."

" Oh !" said Dora, " I'm so sorry."

" Never mind.   I shall have another vessel soon, for I have a mint of money to draw upon.   And if I didn't, I have but to go to the St. George Hotel, or a dozen other places, and ask for a steamer, and I should be overwhelmed with offers."

" Yes," she said, " I'm sure of it."

" And now where's Norah, your fair guest ?"

" Gone."

" Gone?   What do you mean ?"

" She went away an hour ago with a Mr. Bentham —the man she expects to marry."

" Ah, indeed ! I heard he was in Nassau.   He might have trusted her here.   She was perfectly safe."

" He was afraid of Flash Gilmor's persecutions, and Captain Powers also was hot upon his track and hers."

" Gilmor will not trouble Norah, or in fact any one, any more."

" I am glad of that, for I love Norah dearly."

" And I have warned Captain Powers.   But I must see Bentham.   Do you know where he went with the girl ?"

" I think they went to Mr. Throxton's."

" I am almost sure of it.   I will follow them shortly,

my dear. In the meantime I wish you would lay the table for me. I am quite famished. I have tasted nothing for twenty-four hours."

" You dear old uncle, why didn't you speak at first? You know I am so thoughtless."

"I don't know any such thing, Dora," said Powell tenderly, as his niece ran away into the next room.

A repast was soon spread before him, and while he disposed of the good things he thought out his plans in respect to young Bentham, whom he expected to meet now without much difficulty.

What scheme had he in view?

At any rate his thoughts could not have been badly tinged with evil, for his fine bronzed countenance never looked more benign or unruffled than on the present occasion.

CHAPTER XXIX.

AT THE POINT OF THE REVOLVER.

When Captain Dick Powers, of the new and untried privateer Destroyer, recovered from Powell's stunning blows he found himself in a room which he was aware he had never entered before.

His first impulse was to rush out and follow the blockade runner, whom he knew could not be far away.

He would pay Powell back for those blows; he would have his life for them; he would yet carry out his oath by making Norah his wife!

Scrambling to his feet, for he had fallen headlong into the house, he was about to make a dash for the street, when a man stepped suddenly between him and the door, and faced him with determined if not triumphant countenance.

"Throxton!" exclaimed Powers, starting back as he stared at the man, whom he instantly recognized. "I was not aware that I had fallen into your house."

The man at the door seemed to smile maliciously.

"You came in without knocking," he answered. "I was not expecting a visitor—especially an officer in the employ of the Confederacy."

"Which means that I am not welcome."

"Ah! you are mistaken!" was the quick rejoinder. "Of all the men I know, there is not one whom I would rather see here than yourself. When do you sail, Captain Powers?"

Powers' eyes flashed indignantly.

"I generally keep my own secrets, Throxton," he said.

"Very well. We will not press the subject."

For another moment the privateer eyed the Unionist, and then strode toward the door again.

Throxton did not stir.

"Let me out!" exclaimed Powers, seeing that there was a disposition on Throxton's part to detain him. "You have no right to keep me here against my will. You have already incurred the ill-will of the authorities by harboring and hiding Bentham, the Yankee gunner, to-night. I have a right to demand my liberty."

"And as this is my own house I claim the right to refuse it."

"What, sir? This language to an officer who sails under the flag of the Confederate government?" exclaimed Powers. "By Jove! I will put an end to your double game. You have been permitted to escape too long. This act seals your doom—puts an end to your practices, and cripples the Yankee cause."

A light, irritating laugh rippled over Throxton's lips.

"Just as you please, captain," he said, with cutting sarcasm; "but first you must get away from here."

"You will not let me out, then?"

"I will not."

Powell sprang back with an oath, and his hand darted swiftly toward his belt.

"Ho! none of that," said Throxton quietly, but

with firmness, anticipating his design. "One more move of that kind on your part, captain, might cause the Confederacy to lose a very valuable officer. My death would but hasten yours. I have other guests to-night. Come into the parlor and let me introduce them."

"I decline the honor, sir," said Powers haughtily.

"Excuse me if I insist."

Powers debated an instant whether to resort to violence or not, and finally decided not to do so.

He preceded the master of the house into the room in question.

"This way a moment, Robert, with your friend," said Throxton, raising his voice, and addressing some one in another room, the door leading to which stood slightly ajar.

Powers removed his eyes from Throxton and fixed them on the door, which opened, and a handsome man stepped forward.

"Bentham!" fell from Powers' tongue, "I might have known that you were about to appear—and Norah, too!"

The young gunner and beautiful Norah Narcross stood before the Confederate captain.

It was an interesting tableau.

"You got the worst of your encounter with Powell, captain, I see," said the gunner, the first to disturb the silence.

The privateersman's answer was a growl of anger.

"I do not intend to twit you on your defeat," continued Bentham quickly. "You were looking for me awhile ago, and since we have met, let us transact what unfinished business remains."

The young gunner was evidently thinking of the impromptu duel on the banks of Cape Fear, the night of his escape from Wilmington, and while he spoke Captain Powers' look told that his thoughts had returned to the same scene.

"I am willing to accommodate you!" he exclaimed. "Your sword gave me a terrible wound, and your accursed balls sent the Swiftwing to the bowels of the deep. Yes, I want revenge. I acknowledge it here. Mr. Throxton, have you swords for us?"

The Union sympathizer was about to reply when Norah threw herself between the two men, who faced each other with flashing eyes.

"No; blood shall not flow here," she said, looking at Powers, who recoiled a step. "You have not forgotten your vow, captain. It is still fresh in my memory. You shall never fulfill it; for Norah Narcross will never become the wife of a man who serves the new flag."

"I believe you said that once before. Beware, girl! you may recall those words."

"At your hands? never!"

"We'll see! But this is not business," and the speaker looked at the Union gunner again. "The world is too small for both of us, Bentham. I want revenge for my wound and the loss of my ship. Coward, you dare not face me! Having disgraced the man whose money educated you, you stand behind a woman, a branded poltroon, unworthy to serve the flag you own."

An exclamation of anger burst from Bentham's throat. This was too much. He strode toward the privateer with clinched hands and fiery eyes.

Norah looked appealingly to Throxton.

She felt that she could do no more.

" No !" suddenly exclaimed Bentham, halting almost within reach of his waiting enemy. " I shall not touch you, viper. My revenge shall not consist of strokes with hand or blade. Get me writing materials, Throxton."

The Unionist had locked the door and removed the key some time before, so that Powers was safely caged.

He now moved forward, and, lifting the lid of a desk, took from within paper, pens and ink, which he placed at the Union gunner's disposal.

The Confederate privateer looked wonderingly on.

What new indignity was he to be subjected to now?

His lips met firmly as he took a mental resolve not to barter one of his rights away.

He would die rather than sign an oath of allegiance to the United States.

Neither would he put the name of Powers to a parole.

" I will respect your eagerness, and proceed to business, captain," said Bentham, turning from the desk. " Come forward and take up the pen."

" To sign the rights of a Confederate officer away ? —never !" was the flashing rejoinder, and Powers seemed to brace himself more firmly where he stood.

Bentham and Throxton exchanged rapid glances and a sign.

" You will obey Mr. Bentham, captain," said the latter firmly. " Disobedience may cost you more than your rights—life itself !"

" We mean business, sir ;" and he was covered by a revolver, which Throxton had drawn. " Go forward, sir, and take up the pen. Bentham will dictate to you !"

Menaced by the weapon, above which were the cold gray eyes of Throxton—a man who feared nothing—Powers bit his lip and moved forward.

He glared savagely at Bentham, and a muttered curse was heard as he laid hold of the pen.

" Write to your first officer, Jones, now on board the Destroyer, as follows," said Bentham, and he proceeded:

" Mr. Jones : On receipt of this you will turn the command of the ship over to the bearer, and submit to him in every particular. I have been detailed on a secret mission of immediate importance. I shall leave Nassau for a time, but will join you ere long. The bearer of this, Captain Randolph, is a thorough sailor and a devoted Confederate ; therefore he is a man who can be trusted. He will sail from Nassau immediately. I am sure that you will obey him and fight the ship under him as you would fight it with me on the quarter-deck. Remember that the Destroyer is to avenge the Swiftwing. POWERS."

While Bentham spoke, the privateer's pen did not touch the paper.

He straightened his handsome figure, and glared at the Union gunner with the glittering eyes of a jungle tiger.

" This is infamy without a parallel !" he exclaimed, as Bentham concluded. " You would force me to become a traitor to the Confederacy. Who is the man designed to play the rôle of Captain Randolph in this piece of rascality ?"

" He stands before you," answered Bentham, bowing.

" You ! Then, by the stars of heaven ! I will die before I pen a word of the message !" And the next moment the pen was hurled from the incensed Confederate's hand and quivered in the floor.

Throxton advanced a stride.

"Write or die, captain!" he said, in tones not to be mistaken. "We do not intend to trifle in this matter. Repeat the message, Bentham. He will sign!"

Powers hesitated for a moment, during which time he glanced from Throxton to the young gunner, who stood ready to carry out the Unionist's command.

All at once he stooped and tore the pen from the carpet.

"This triumph will not last!" he grated, fixing his eyes for a moment on Bentham. "Carry your infamy through to the end, Robert Bentham. I swear that you shall never tread the Destroyer's quarter-deck as her commander!"

With the last word he turned to the paper on the desk, and waited for Bentham's dictation.

"There, you are satisfied now!" he exclaimed, when he had written the last word and turned upon Bentham. "You have triumphed; but the game has not been played through. I am free now?"

He strode toward the door as he concluded.

"Not yet. We must detain you here, captain," said Throxton.

The privateer groaned.

"I am a prisoner still?" he said.

"Yes."

"For how long?"

"Until after the Destroyer, with Captain Randolph, has sailed," smiled Bentham.

There was no reply.

If Powers' glance could have killed at that moment, Bentham would have fallen dead in his tracks.

CHAPTER XXX.

'TWIXT LOVE AND DUTY.

" JUPE," exclaimed Bentham.

" Here I is, Marse Bob," said the darky, making his appearance.

" Take Captain Powers upstairs to the back room, and mount guard outside."

" All right, sah. Cap'n Powers, I will take great pleasure, sah, in showin' you'se ter de uppah floor. I is 'ticlar perlite ter a gen'l'man ob yer rank an' stashun in de Confed'rate service, an' I hope dat you'se won't 'blige me ter 'sist yer locomotion wid any pers'nal 'tention."

Powers glared at Jupe, and then concealing his great chagrin under an assumption of dignity, he folded his arms and followed his conductor.

" Now, Bentham," said Throxton, " after this affair Nassau will be too hot for me as well as yourself. My daughter and I will pack our things. I think you had better get on board the Destroyer as soon as you can and assume command. Send a boat to the landing in an hour for Norah, my daughter, Jupe and myself. We will be ready."

" All right, Throxton."

" I need not tell you that it would be advisable to have steam up and everything ready for departure."

" Certainly. I will now go to your room and disguise myself. It is lucky you have taken precautions in my behalf in this direction. My own face, you know, would never pass master on the privateer, for one of Powers' petty officers and several of the crew have already seen me."

At this moment a loud rap came at the door.

Throxton peeped out through the blinds.

"Here's a complication," he said.

"What do you mean?"

"Who do you suppose seeks admission here?"

"I have no idea."

"Captain Powell."

"The devil! He must not suspect our purpose. I will get out of the way, and do you get rid of him as best you can."

A second knock, louder and more peremptory than the first, accelerated Bentham's exit from the room.

As soon as the young gunner was out of sight Throxton opened the door and confronted the late commander of the Foxhound.

"Good-evening, Mr. Throxton," said Powell, "may I ask if Bob Bentham and Norah Mowbray are in your house?"

"Miss Mowbray is here, Captain Powell; but Bentham went away a short time since. Were he here I should hardly think he would care to see you."

Powell was clearly disappointed.

"He need not fear me, Throxton. I won't cause him any trouble."

"He does not fear for himself. His mission to Nassau was on his sweetheart's account, and now that I have taken charge of her, he expects to leave town immediately."

"My niece thinks a good deal of Miss Mowbray," said Powell.

"The feeling is reciprocated, captain, I assure you. Miss Mowbray says that your niece Dora is the sweetest girl she ever met."

Captain Powell was evidently gratified at this intelligence, and after a pause said he would call again perhaps.

Powell did not return to his own house but walked down the street.

Ten minutes later Bentham, attired as the pseudo Captain Randolph, slipped out of the house and took his way toward the water front.

He found one of the steamer's boats at the mole.

It was waiting for Captain Dick Powers, according to orders.

It had been there some time, and the officer in charge had grown very impatient.

"I wish to go on board the Destroyer," said Bentham politely.

"Who are you, sir?" asked the officer in surly tones.

"Captain Randolph, of the Confederate navy. I am to take charge of the steamer pending Captain Powers' absence."

"You are?" said the petty officer in sarcastic tones.

"That's what I said, sir."

"You be blowed! You can tell that to the marines."

"Sir!" exclaimed Bentham with dignity.

"You needn't put on airs," said the officer. "I don't know you, sir, and what's more I don't want to. This boat is waiting for Cap'n Powers, and if you wait long enough you'll see him."

"Perhaps if you will look at this note. directed to Mr. Jones, your first officer, you will see that I speak the truth."

The officer became civil at once as soon as he perceived the letter with the superscription.

"Captain Powers is not going aboard to-night then?" he said, without opening the note.

"I am to act for the time being in Captain Powers' stead. I wish to go aboard at once."

"Very, well, cap'n—what did you say your name is?"

"Randolph."

"All right, Cap'n Randolph, we'll shove off at once."

On their way they passed the blockade runner Seabird, on board which the reader will remember Jupe had his short but exciting adventure.

She had steam up, a rather portentous indication of an early departure.

Captain Nugent, however, was ashore looking up his friend Flash Gilmor.

In a few minutes Bentham was alongside of the Destroyer, and he had a fair view of the new privateer.

She was a powerful iron vessel, pierced for a broadside of six guns, was painted lead color, and her two masts had a decided rake.

On deck our hero made out an Armstrong rifled gun on the forecastle, and another and much more formidable one in the waist, just forward of the funnel, precisely as was located his own Parrott gun on board of the Avenger.

Altogether she was an ugly customer—abundantly prepared to beat off a great many of Uncle Sam's cruisers.

Indeed, if well manned and handled, was likely to hold her own against the Avenger, which vessel was acknowledged to be one of the best American screw war steamers.

The counterfeit Captain Randolph presented his letter to Mr. Jones on the quarter-deck.

He was politely received, and duly vested with the authority of commander *pro tem.*

"Now, Mr. Jones," said the disguised Bentham. "How long will it take you to get under way."

"One hour, Cap'n Randolph."

"All hands are aboard, I believe?"

"Yes, sir; we expected to sail at any moment."

"Very well; get on a head of steam at once. And, by the way, send a boat to the mole. There is a. gentleman, his servant, and two ladies coming off."

Mr. Jones looked his surprise.

"I am to deliver them under flag of truce to the first Yankee cruiser we sight."

This explanation satisfied the first officer and he gave orders to send the boat.

The hour had nearly elapsed and Bentham was watching for the return of the boat when the steamer was hailed from the port side.

"Hallo, there, what do you want?" said a petty officer.

"Want ter come on board, boss."

"Keep away—you can't board this craft."

"Must do it, Massa Ossifer. Got a message from Cap'n Powers ter Cap'n Randolph."

"Hand it up, then, quick."

"Can't do it, sah; must see de cap'n myself. Berry 'ticklar."

"Come aboard, then."

"All right, sah. Be up in a twist ob a cat's tail."

In a moment who should come over the rail but Jupe.

"Berry kind ob you, sah. Whar's de cap'n ?"

"Come with me."

" 'Spects I will, sah."

The petty officer spoke to Mr. Jones and said the negro had a message from Captain Powers for the new commander.

Jupe was brought to Bentham, who was both disturbed and astounded by his unexpected appearance.

"In heaven's name, Jupe !" he whispered, "what's wrong."

" 'Spects eberyting am wrong. You'se better get out ob here quick'rn greased lightnin', Massa Bob, or you'll be gobbled up for suah."

"Explain yourself."

"Cap'n Powers done escaped from dat yer room, sah. I found it out, an' follered him. I cotched him near de square and fetched him a berry fine crack in de jaw dat knocked him endwise all ob a heap. Den I put fer de mole in a hurry, Marse Bob, fer a crowd got 'bout de cap'n, an' it would hab been mighty hot fer dis yer chile ter stay in dat yer locality. I reckon dat he won't recubber from dat jawbreaker fer a while, but you'se ain't got a speck ob time ter spare. Start de engine an' get away, sah, or you'll be cotched fer sartin."

"And leave Norah, and the others behind, Jupe? Impossible !"

"Den de jig'll be up, sah. I reckon dat it's yer duty, Marse Bob, now dat you'se got de chance, to take dis yer steamer whar de Stars an' Stripes 'll float above her. I reckon dat she's a berry bad customer under de Confed'rate flag. If dat Cap'n Powers get aboard she'll do a heap ob damage somewbar ag'in de Yankees. I guess Marse Bob knows his duty, sah."

"Yes, Jupe," said Bentham, after an effort. " It was a stuggle between love and duty, but my country wins. May heaven preserve my Norah from harm, and may Throxton forgive me for deserting him! I have but one course—and I will act on it."

He issued his instructions to man the windlass and get under way.

"The boat you ordered sent ashore has not returned," said Mr. Jones.

"Never mind the boat now. We must leave without an instant's delay. My orders are imperative."

Mr. Jones said nothing, though he looked his surprise.

In a brief time the chain was all in, the anchor catted, and the Destroyer was steaming out of the harbor.

A few persons on the mole watched her departure, and mentally wished her Godspeed, for their hearts beat for the Confederacy.

There was scarcely any commotion on her decks, and before a great while she had left the lights of Nassau far behind.

All at once the occupants of the mole were startled by a man who rushed frantically to the water's edge, and stared seaward like a madman.

"Too late!" he fairly groaned. "They have carried the infamous conspiracy out to the letter. The Destroyer will be sailing under the infernal Yankee flag in less than twenty-four hours."

His manner and voice attracted everybody.

They gathered around him.

"Captain Powers!" exclaimed several. "We thought you were on board the Destroyer."

"Would I be here if I was?" was the answer. "I am the victim of one of the most infamous conspiracies on record. A Yankee sailor commands the Destroyer. You can guess what his intentions are."

"Who is he?" asked a voice that made Powers start. Captain Powell confronted him.

"Who but Bentham," said the baffled privateersman. "Curse you, Powell! If it had not been for you this infamous scheme would never have been consummated."

The speaker glared fiercely at the blockade runner.

"So, Bob Bentham has eloped with the Destroyer, eh?" laughed Captain Powell sardonically. "By Jove! This is the hugest joke of the war!"

"Joke? It's a lasting stain on the Confederate navy!"

"I can't see how the scheme was carried out."

"I was secured by Throxton and Bentham after a desperate resistance and compelled to sign an infamous order to my first officer, directing him to turn the command of my steamer over to the bearer," said Captain Powers, the last word ending with a hiss. "Having secured the paper, I was then detained a prisoner in order to give the conspirators the opportunity to put their plot through. I effected my escape a short time ago and came straight here, only to discover that I am too late."

"Rather rough on you," said Powell.

"Rough!—but no matter. You can do your country a service, Ralph Powell."

"How?"

"By getting afloat at once, pursuing the Destroyer and recapturing her.

"That is impossible, Powers. I have no ship. You have forgotten that the Foxhound is at the bottom of the sea."

For a moment longer the two captains looked at one another, then Powers held out his hand.

"We need not be foes. I forgive you all your blows, Powell," he said. "Let us combine."

The blockade runner drew his form up haughtily, and answered savagely, as he turned away:

"Combine with you—with a man who let a Yankee steal a ship—never!" he said. "I have too much respect for the cause I serve, Captain Powers. Fight your own battles, but I would warn you to be careful how you cross Bentham's path. He learned more than gunnery on the continent."

Powers' mad look followed the blockade runner until he passed out of his sight, when, almost bursting with rage, he wheeled to leave the mole, when he came face to face with Captain Nugent.

After some parleying, the blockade runner agreed to take Captain Powers on the Seabird in pursuit of the Destroyer. It would only be necessary to get within hail and make himself known to his officers and crew. They would then put the impostor in irons and restore their proper commander to his place.

CHAPTER XXXI.

A STRATAGEM OF WAR.

Black and angry-looking clouds hung over the heavens like a pall and a nasty sea was running, through which the Seabird pitched and rolled heavily.

She had run along without mishap for several hours through foggy, squally weather, hugging the shore closely. One suspicious vessel, probably a Yankee cruiser, had come in sight, but the fleet Seabird had easily distanced her.

"I'm afraid this will prove a dangerous mission for me," said Captain Nugent, as he paced the deck with Captain Powers. "I've got a snug cargo of Enfield rifles and a power of cartridges aboard. I'd make a pretty prize for the Yankees, and I fear there's more chance of falling in with a cruiser than meeting the Destroyer."

Before Powers could reply the lookout signaled a steamer was dead ahead.

The stranger ahead showed a clear light, and might therefore be reckoned a war vessel without the conjecture going very wide of its mark.

"What do you think of her?" asked Captain Nugent anxiously.

"I can't say," replied Powers, who was staring through the night-glass, "but I hope it's the Destroyer. We ought to fetch her about this time."

"I fear it's a Yankee."

"I hope you'll crawl up and investigate," said

Powers, who entertained some doubts as to Nugent's intentions since the narrow shave the Seabird had from the cruiser.

"I'll go on a bit. We show no light of any kind and lie low in the water. Since I've gone into this thing I'm willing to take some chances, but you must understand I can't afford to lose my vessel, even to assist the Confederacy."

"You are the master here and I must bow to whatever you decide upon; but I believe there is a reasonable chance for judging that yonder craft is my vessel. I can recognize the Destroyer if you will go near enough to afford me a plain view."

"I will go as close to her as I dare," said Nugent frankly, and Captain Powers felt that that was all he could reasonably expect of the blockade runner.

It was certainly a risky venture, though everything favored the little lead-colored steamer.

The vessel ahead was under moderate speed, so that the Seabird crept rapidly up to the windward.

Captain Powers was visibly excited.

He was more than half-assured that the blot on the water, a couple of points off the starboard bow, was the wished-for Destroyer.

"What's our course?" he inquired.

Nugent consulted the binnacle, which was shaded so that the light could not be seen seaward, and returned to Powers.

"East by east-sou'-east," he said.

"The weather has thickened so that I can't get a good view of the steamer," said Powers, "but we're coming up very fast. I should like to chance a private signal pretty soon, if you'll allow me. If it's the Destroyer, she'll answer it. Bentham couldn't prevent it without raising immediate suspicion."

"You may do so," said Nugent, after a moment's reflection.

"Thank you," said Captain Powers.

Half an hour passed, and during the interval it began to rain heavily.

The stranger was almost lost sight of for awhile.

At last the rain let up and the weather grew much clearer.

The steamer was now within three miles and plainly to be made out by aid of the glass.

"I could swear it's the Destroyer," said Powers, after a good look. "Send a man up the fore-rigging with a red lantern, and another at his heels with a blue one, and let off steam three times for half a minute, with two intervals between."

The directions given by Captain Powers were carried out exactly.

After the lapse of a few minutes, three red lights appeared in the stranger's rigging in the form of a triangle.

"It's the Destroyer!" exclaimed Powers, almost hugging Nugent in his glee. "Now, Bob Bentham, this farce will soon end! Unless you jump overboard before I reach yonder deck I'll hang you higher than Haman of old!"

"Steamer on port bow!" sung out the lookout.

So engrossed had all hands been with the stranger ahead that no one thought of looking for another vessel.

The watch aloft, whose duty it was to discover any vessel as soon as she hove in sight, had certainly been neglectful in his duty, for the second steamer was close aboard off the Seabird's quarter, and had evidently run out of the mist that was slowly clearing away.

At that moment a rocket soared upward from the Destroyer's bow and burst into a myriad of sparks.

"What the devil can that mean?" exclaimed Powers. "It's very strange."

The newcomer, which was heading directly for the Seabird, now altered her course several points and edged down for the privateer ahead.

"Great Scott!" cried Powers, after he had examined her dark, heaving hull through his glass. "It's the Avenger. I thought she was leagues away. Put on full steam, Nugent; we must reach the Destroyer first."

"It's too risky, Powers. I never could put you aboard your craft in this sea, and get away myself. I'm in range of the Yankee as it is. All that saved us, if we are safe, was that rocket from your own vessel. You'd better give up and trust the rest to chance. Your vessel is not yet lost. Bentham will have to fight his own ship or be exposed, and I guess that would settle his goose."

Powers made no reply—he was far too excited at the sudden change in the aspect of affairs, and Captain Nugent took advantage of the diversion to change the course of his steamer.

He determined to sneak out of harm's way if he could.

Powers noticed the variation in the Seabird's course and remonstrated.

"I've taken all the risk I can afford," said Nugent decidedly. "To go further will be to throw away my vessel and cargo. I'm off to Charleston in earnest. Take my advice, Powers—trust to luck."

Captain Nugent was master of his own steamer, and having decided upon his line of action, nothing that Powers said made the faintest impression on him.

The Seabird was now headed N. E. by N. and going ahead at top speed, increasing her distance every moment from the Yankee cruiser, who paid her no further attention, but bore down on the Destroyer.

*　　*　　*　　*　　*

We will return to Robert Bentham and the faithful Jube.

The latter had been turned over to Mr. Jones, who sent him forward to mess with the crew.

Jupe had received secret instructions from the *soi-disant* Captain Randolph as to the part he might be expected to play in the impending drama.

He carried on his person a signal rocket which he was to discharge from the privateer's bow at the proper moment.

It was an act that bristled with danger, for was his agency in the affair discovered, he might better jump into the sea than face the exasperated crew.

Bentham's situation was one of peril and difficulty.

He had to so perform his hazardous mission that no suspicion of his true character should be evident to the astute Mr. Jones, or any other quarter-deck officer.

He was surrounded by watchful eyes, and an error of judgment might cost him his life on the spot.

Meanwhile the Destroyer got fairly to sea, and under half-speed was churning her way through foam and spray.

As soon as Great Abaco light was fairly seen on the

port beam, Bentham went below and coolly took possession of Captain Powers' stateroom.

There were several Yankee cruisers on the station,
but not one had been sighted up to the instant he had
quitted the deck.

The clouds were opaque above, with a heavy sea below, and a dense mist around, and the general prospect
not encouraging to the young gunner, though quite
satisfactory to everybody else, if we except Jupe, in
the ship.

The negro was very alert and active on the main
gun-deck.

He glided from gun to gun, pausing at each for a
while, and paying great attention to the breech of the
weapon.

What was he doing?

His movements escaped notice, and by and by he went
on the upper deck and crawled under the tarpaulin that
protected the huge Armstrong rifle amidships.

Some time afterward he might have been seen on
the rise of the forecastle, where the wicked-looking
bow-chaser was snugly wrapped in its canvas overcoat.

After that Jupe clung persistently to the waist of
the privateer, and sought shelter from the rain and
spray under the cover of the pivot rifle, but maintained
a position where he could easily command a view of the
quarter-deck.

Bentham was below when a steamer was reported
about five miles dead astern, and he immediately went
on deck.

This was the Seabird, as already described, but her

identity was unknown to any one on board the privateer.

The general impression prevailed for a time that the
craft, which was rapidly overhauling them, was a Yankee
cruiser.

Finally, when the mist and rain dissolved and the
atmosphere cleared, Powers' signal created a decided
sensation.

Mr. Jackson, the second officer, had charge of the
deck, and he duly reported the signal, the import of
which was read to mean: "Lay to till we speak
you."

Bentham received the intelligence without a quiver,
and coolly directed Jackson to return a suitable answer.

Directly afterward the second steamer seen from
the Seabird's deck shot into view out of the mist bank
fast receding to the westward, and Bentham, fully alive
to his desperate situation, gave the signal to Jupe, who
at once crawled forward to the forecastle, dropped
into the chains and sent up the rocket, which, if the
stranger was a Yankee war-vessel, as seemed likely,
would be understood at once.

The sending up of the rocket caused great commotion
on board the Destroyer, for it was evidently a signal
to the enemy, who was observed to change her course
and stand directly for the privateer.

Bentham watched her approach with anxiety.

As she drew near her appearance grew more and more
familiar to him, until finally he felt assured that she was
his own ship the Avenger, which he thought was miles
and miles away on her regular mission.

Bentham now observed that the first steamer—the one

which had signaled a short time before—had altered her course and was steaming away to the northward.

As the Avenger approached, Bentham, to maintain his character, was compelled to clear the steamer for action, and every preparation was made for a desperate fight.

At this point in affairs a great outcry arose from the gun-deck.

An officer hurriedly appeared on the quarter-deck and announced that the vents of all the guns had been tampered with—not seriously, but enough to cause delay and a feeling of exasperation against the perpetrator.

The impression, caused by the discharge of the rocket, that there was a traitor on board, was now confirmed, and the crew were furious.

Dire threats of vengeance prevailed.

Bentham without hesitation ordered a thorough search "of the vessel, and while this was going on a second rocket went up from the privateer's bows, to the consternation of all on board.

The usual signal for name and number was displayed by the Yankee in her rigging, but merely as a preliminary to the shot which immediately followed from her bow-chaser.

While many of the Confederate crew were making things hum on the forecastle, trying to discover the traitor who had done the signaling, a blue light sprang into a flame on the bulwark rail just under the break of the poop.

The crew of the Armstrong rifle rushed to the side as one man and extinguished it. While they were doing this a crash came up from the engine-room, the machinery stopped, and the privateer rolled slowly from side to side on the heaving sea.

Crash!

A shot from the Avenger's heavy Parrott gun smashed in the weather bulwark and struck the carriage of the Armstrong rifle, jamming the gearing so that the gun could not be worked on its traversing-platform.

The greatest excitement prevailed.

The Avenger continued to approach rapidly, firing her bow gun and forward battery.

The assistant-engineer reported to the pseudo Captain Randolph that the chief engineer had been stunned by some one who had come upon him unawares, and who then threw a heavy steel bar, which was used in the engine-room, among the rods, causing a smash-up that could not be repaired for hours.

Bentham's indignation was admirably assumed.

He had already dispatched the second and third officers to search the steamer.

He now sent Mr. Jones down into the engine-room, and walked to the break of the poop.

Jupe was apparently assisting the crew of the Armstrong gun, who were trying to extricate the carriage from the difficulty it was in.

Bentham called him to the quarter-deck, and sent him with hurried instructions to the wheel.

Jupe slipped quickly behind the helmsman, and lifting him in his powerful embrace, tore him from his hold on the spokes and tossed him overboard.

He then jammed the wheel hard down, bringing the Destroyer up into the wind's eye, so that her broadside would not bear upon the Avenger, which had ceased firing and was close aboard on the privateer's port quarter.

"What steamer is that?" roared Captain Graham from the mizzen rigging of the cruiser.

"Confederate steamer Destroyer," shouted Bentham. "Pipe away your boats and take possession—quick!"

No doubt Captain Graham was astonished with the general character of the reply, but he lost no time in issuing orders.

The Avenger held a raking position.

The boatswain's whistle came lustily down on the wind, three boats were lowered and the crews were soon over the side and into the launches in true man-o'-war style.

The boats danced over the water quickly, but the Confederate crew, not having understood their quarter-deck reply to the Yankee's hail, were preparing for a desperate resistance.

"It's useless, my men," said Bentham, looking down upon such of the crew as were ready to repel boarders. "We have been betrayed and must surrender. Yonder craft can sweep us from stern to stern. Look at his guns run out, and the men hold the lanyards ready. We can't help ourselves."

The crew were thunderstruck and their demoralization was complete.

Mr. Jones at that moment rushed up from the engine-room and sprang upon the quarter-deck.

"What's the meaning of this, Captain Randolph? Treachery has ruined us. The machinery is wrecked. Our guns have been tampered with, and signal rockets discharged. I believe that infernal nigger is at the bottom of this!"

He drew his revolver, but Bentham arrested his arm.

"Don't be rash, Mr. Jones."

"Rash, sir!" exclaimed the Confederate officer, turning upon him in a rage. "It's my opinion you're the cause of all this."

Bentham made no reply.

"In the devil's name who are you?" cried the officer.

"Bob Bentham, of the United States cruiser Avenger yonder, and you are my prisoner!"

Bentham tore off his false beard.

"Then your life shall pay forfeit for your treachery!" cried Mr. Jones.

"Jupe!"

The negro sprang upon the Confederate officer just as Lieutenant Haskins of the Avenger's first cutter sprang over the stern rail, where the negro had thrown ropes to afford means of ascent to the cutter's crew.

At the same moment the Destroyer was boarded at the waist and at the chains forward.

In a twinkling forty jack tars were on deck driving the disorganized Confederate crew below.

"Bentham!" exclaimed Lieutenant Haskins, hardly believing his eyes.

"Ay, ay, sir," touching his cap. "I take great pleasure in turning over to you the possession of the Confederate privateer Destroyer."

"Treacherous hound!" exclaimed Mr. Jones, as he lay upon the deck encircled by Jupe's arms, "you shall hang some day for this!"

"Thank you," said Bob Bentham politely. "I'll take the risk."

Having seen Bentham, the gallant young gunner, triumphant in one of the shrewdest games of the whole war, the story is almost told.

But how happened it that the Avenger, which had been bound southward, came to turn up so opportunely at her old cruising ground?

Captain Graham had touched at Havana, where he found an order from the secretary of war calling his attention to the fact that the department had been advised of the fitting out at Nassau of a new and dangerous privateer called the Destoyer, which was to be entrusted to Captain Powers, late commander of the Swiftwing.

The order directed Graham to return to the Bahamas and head her off, which he did, with the result we have already detailed.

Bentham was dispatched home in the captured privateer, which was in command of the Avenger's second officer as prize master. He wore a lieutenant's uniform when he rejoined the Avenger, and a commander's at the close of the war; but long before the happy termination of the conflict he was united in marriage to the girl of his heart—Norah Narcross, otherwise Mowbray.

The large estate left by Gordon Mowbray was confiscated on a technicality by the Confederate government; but at the end of the war, Bentham instituted legal proceedings and recovered for his wife a portion of her property.

As for Powell, the blockade runner, he served the Confederacy in that capacity to the close of the war, and many was the rich cargo he bore across the seas to the lost cause.

Jupe, the faithful black, remained with Bentham to

the close of the terrible conflict, and served the Union bravely in many a desperate encounter afloat and ashore.

It seems that the letter which so mysteriously reached Bentham after the great naval fight in Hampton Roads had been intrusted to a slave for delivery, but something frightened the messenger so that, instead of placing it in Bentham's hands, he left it under the bastion where it was found and served its purpose.

The loyal Throxton, of course, never returned to Nassau after his escape with the gunner in the Destroyer. If he had he would have been seized and summarily dealt with.

Powers and Powell would have hunted him down.

He entered the Union service before the close of the war, serving under Bentham, who commanded the Avenger at the close of hostilities. He was rewarded for his services at Nassau.

Dora, Powell's niece, married a Confederate captain, and Jennie Throxton found a lover and husband in the person of a young Union officer.

Peace hovers over land and sea, and bestows her laurels upon friend and foe alike—whether they trod the decks of a Union brig, or manned the guns of a Confederate sloop-of-war.

[THE END.]